Published by arrangement with La Galera, S.A. Editorial.
Originally published in Catalan by La Galera
under the title "La caputxeta vermella"

Bilingual version supervised by SUR Editorial Group, Inc.
English translation by James Surges.
Bilingual typesetting and cover design by Vandy Ritter.
Typeset in Weiss and Handle Old Style.
Printed in Hong Kong.
ISBN: 0-8118-2562-0 (pb) 0-8118-2561-2 (hc)

Library of Congress Cataloging-in-Publication Data
Rotkåppchen, English & Spanish
Little Red Riding Hood = Caperucita roja / by the Brothers Grimm ;
illustrated by Pau Estrada.
p. cm.
Summary: A little girl meets a hungry wolf in the forest while on her
way to visit her sick grandmother.
[1. Fairy tales. 2. Folklore—Germany. 3. Spanish language materials—
Bilingual.] I. Grimm, Jacob, 1785–1863. II. Grimm, Wilhelm, 1786–1859.
III. Estrada, Pau, ill. IV. Little Red Riding Hood. English & Spanish. V.
Title. VI. Title: Caperucita roja.
PZ74.R68 1999
398.2'094302—dc21
99-21354
CIP

Distributed in Canada by Raincoast Books
9050 Shaughnessy Street, Vancouver, British Columbia V6P 6E5

10 9 8 7 6 5 4 3 2

Chronicle Books LLC
85 Second Street, San Francisco, California 94105
www.chroniclebooks.com/Kids

Little Red Riding Hood

Caperucita Roja

By The Brothers Grimm
Illustrated by Pau Estrada

chronicle books · san francisco

Once upon a time, there lived a little girl called Little Red Riding Hood.
Everyone loved her, but it was her grandmother who loved her most of all. One day her grandmother made her a riding hood of red velvet. The girl liked the gift so much that she never took it off. And that's why people called her Little Red Riding Hood.

~

Había una vez una niña llamada Caperucita Roja.
Todo el mundo la quería mucho, pero su abuelita era la que más la quería. Un día, su abuelita le hizo una caperuza de terciopelo rojo. A la niña le quedaba tan bien que nunca se la quitaba. Por eso todos la llamaban Caperucita Roja.

One day her mother said to her,
"Here, Little Red Riding Hood, I want you to take this basket to Grandmother. There's a jar of honey and a pie inside. Be very careful when you go into the forest. Head straight to your grandmother's house and don't dally along the way." Grandmother lived far off in the heart of the forest.

Un día su madre le dijo:

—Caperucita, quiero que vayas a ver a la abuela para llevarle esta cesta. Dentro hay una jarrita de miel y un pastel. Pero ten mucho cuidado cuando entres en el bosque: ve derecho a casa de la abuelita y no te entretengas por el camino.

La abuelita vivía muy lejos en el corazón del bosque.

When Little Red Riding Hood reached the forest, the wolf came out to meet her and said,

"Hello there, Little Red Riding Hood. Where are you off to so early?"

"I'm going to Grandmother's house. She isn't well, and I'm taking her this jar of honey and a pie."

"Where does your grandmother live?"

"She lives far off in the forest, in the house beneath the three oaks."

Cuando Caperucita llegó al bosque, el lobo salió a su encuentro y le dijo:

—Hola, Caperucita, ¿adónde vas tan temprano?

—Voy a ver a mi abuelita, que no se siente bien. Le llevo una jarrita de miel y un pastel.

—¿Dónde vive tu abuelita?

—Vive en el bosque muy lejos, en la casa que está bajo los tres encinos.

The wolf thought, "I'll eat well today if I hurry! First the grandmother and then the little girl for dessert. She's a tender morsel, I'll bet!"

But out loud, he said, "You're in such a hurry, Little Red Riding Hood. You don't even notice how beautiful the forest is. Look! Look at the flowers of every color, hear the birds that sing in the treetops, see the rays of sun that shine through the leaves."

"It is beautiful," the girl agreed. And she added, "I'll just gather some flowers for Grandmother. She loves them so much."

She began to pick flowers, while listening to the birds singing in the treetops, and admiring the rays of sun shining through the leaves.

"Good-bye, Little Red Riding Hood," said the wolf.

And while the girl picked flowers, he ran off toward her grandmother's house.

"Si me apuro, hoy comeré muy bien," pensó el lobo. "Primero me comeré a la abuelita y de postre a la niña, ¡que debe estar muy tiernecita!"

—Ibas muy rápido, Caperucita —dijo el lobo en voz alta—. Ni te has dado cuenta de lo bonito que es el bosque. Aquí hay flores de todos los colores, pájaros que cantan en los árboles y los rayos del sol que juguetean entre las hojas…

—¡Es cierto! —respondió la niña. Y luego añadió: —Haré un ramillete para la abuelita porque le gustan mucho las flores.

Y empezó a cortar flores mientras escuchaba el canto de los pájaros y admiraba el brillo del sol entre las hojas.

—Adiós, Caperucita —dijo el lobo.

Y aprovechó que la niña se habia quedado recogiendo flores, para correr hacia la casa de la abuela.

The wolf knocked at the door.

"Who is it?" Grandmother asked.

Putting on a high voice, the wolf said,

"It's Little Red Riding Hood. I've brought you a jar of honey and a pie."

"Come in, come in. The door is open. I'm not well, and I can't get out of bed."

～

El lobo llamó a la puerta.

—¿Quién es? —preguntó la abuela.

Y el lobo, afinando la voz, dijo:

—Soy Caperucita Roja. Te traigo una jarrita de miel y un pastel.

—Entra, entra. La puerta está abierta. Yo estoy enferma y no puedo moverme de la cama.

The wolf opened the door, ran to Grandmother, and GULP! swallowed her whole.

Then he put on her nightgown and sleeping cap and climbed into her bed to wait for the little girl.

———

El lobo abrió la puerta, corrió hacia la abuela y, ¡ZAS!, se la tragó de un solo bocado.

Después se vistió con el camisón y el gorro de dormir de la abuela y se metió en la cama a esperar a que llegara la niña.

Before long, Little Red Riding Hood arrived at the little house beneath the three oaks, carrying a pretty bunch of flowers.

She thought it was a little strange that the door was standing open.

"It's me, Grandmother. Little Red Riding Hood," she called.

But no one answered.

Al poco tiempo, Caperucita Roja llegó a la casita bajo los tres encinos, con un hermoso ramo de flores en la mano.

Le extrañó un poco encontrar la puerta abierta.

—Soy yo, abuelita. Caperucita —dijo en voz alta.

Pero nadie contestó.

Little Red Riding Hood stepped slowly inside.
When she saw Grandmother in bed, she said,
"Why Grandmother! What big ears you have!"
"The better to hear you with."
"Why Grandmother! What big eyes you have!"
"The better to see you with."
"Why Grandmother! What great big teeth you have!"

Caperucita se acercó poco a poco a la cama de la abuela y al verla le dijo:
—¡Ay, abuelita! ¡Qué orejas tan grandes tienes!
—Son para oírte mejor.
—¡Ay, abuelita! ¡Qué ojos tan grandes tienes!
—Son para verte mejor.
—¡Ay, abuelita! ¡Qué dientes tan grandes tienes!

"The better to eat you with!"

And with that the wolf snatched up Little Red Riding Hood and GULP! swallowed her whole. Sleepy after such a large meal, he lay down for a nap and began snoring away.

—¡Es para comerte mejor!

Y entonces el lobo atrapó a la niña y, ¡ZAS!, se tragó a Caperucita de un solo bocado.

Satisfecho después de una comida tan abundante, el lobo se echó a dormir y empezó a roncar.

It so happened that a hunter was passing by.

"My goodness," he thought, "how the old woman is snoring today!
I wonder if she's ill."

———

Pero por suerte, pasaba por allí un cazador.

"Caramba" pensó. "¡Cómo ronca hoy la viejecita! ¿Será que está enferma?"

The hunter went into the house and saw the wolf asleep.

"Aha! Now I've got you, you scoundrel!"
He took up Grandmother's big scissors, cut open the wolf's belly, and out came the relieved and grateful Grandmother and Little Red Riding Hood.

"How terrible it was in there! So dark!" cried the girl. She ran out and came back with two big stones. She stuffed them into the wolf's open belly and closed it up again, sewing it shut, good and tight.

El cazador entró a la casa y vio al lobo dormido.

—Al fin te encuentro, malvado. ¡Ahora verás la que te espera!

El cazador tomó las enormes tijeras de la abuelita, le abrió la panza al lobo y de allí salieron contentas la abuela y Caperucita.

—¡Qué miedo! ¡Estaba todo tan oscuro! —dijo la niña y se fue corriendo a buscar dos grandes piedras. Las metió en la barriga abierta del lobo y la volvió a cerrar, cosiéndola bien cosida.

When the wolf awoke, he jumped up to run away, but the weight of the stones brought him down. The wolf fell dead on the spot, never to rise again.

Little Red Riding Hood, Grandmother and the hunter were very happy. The hunter kept the wolf's fur, Grandmother shared the honey and the pie, and Little Red Riding Hood went straight home, without dallying along the way.

Cuando el lobo despertó, dio un salto para salir corriendo, pero el peso de las piedras le hizo caerse y allí mismo quedó muerto para siempre.

Caperucita, la abuela y el cazador se pusieron muy contentos. El cazador le quitó la piel al lobo, la abuela compartió la miel y el pastel, y después Caperucita Roja se fue derecho a su casa, sin detenerse en el camino.

Also in this series:

Jack and the Beanstalk

Goldilocks and the Three Bears

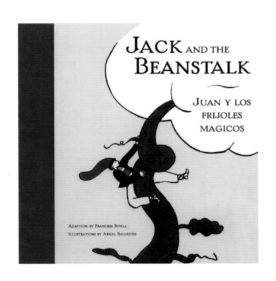 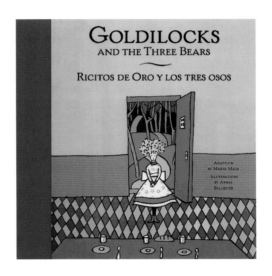

También en esta serie:

Juan y los frijoles mágicos

Ricitos de Oro y los tres osos

DATE DUE

THEY SAW THE FUTURE

ORACLES, PSYCHICS, SCIENTISTS,

GREAT THINKERS,

AND PRETTY GOOD GUESSERS

by

KATHLEEN KRULL

Illustrated by

KYRSTEN BROOKER

An Anne Schwartz Book

ATHENEUM BOOKS FOR YOUNG READERS

To the psychic quilters:
Donna Keefe, Lauriel Adsit, Pam Fruehwirth,
Susan Ghirardi, and Amy Stroot
—K. K.

For Danny, Sarah & Seven Page
—K. B.

I am grateful for the help from Anne Schwartz; Robert Burnham; Larry Dane Brimner, Jane Washburn, and John Miller; Grace Tower, Travis Tidwell, Mary Tajedini, and Loralee Scaiffe; and Denise Diano at Papalulu's. —K. K.

Atheneum Books for Young Readers
An imprint of Simon & Schuster Children's Publishing Division
1230 Avenue of the Americas
New York, New York 10020
Text copyright © 1999 by Kathleen Krull
Illustration copyright © 1999 by Kyrsten Brooker
Book design by Lee Wade
The text of this book is set in Venetian Bold.
The illustrations are rendered in collage and oil paints.
First Edition
Printed in the United States of America
10 9 8 7 6 5 4 3 2 1
Library of Congress Cataloging-in-Publication Data
Krull, Kathleen.
They saw the future: oracles, psychics, scientists, great thinkers, and pretty good guessers /
by Kathleen Krull; illustrated by Kyrsten Brooker.—1st ed.
p. cm.
"An Anne Schwartz book."
Includes bibliographical references and index.
Summary: Discusses the work and predictions of those who have speculated about or claimed to see the future, from the oracles of ancient Greece to such modern figures as Edgar Cayce and Jeane Dixon.
ISBN 0-689-81295-7
1. Prophets—History—Juvenile literature. 2. Prophecies—History—Juvenile literature. 3. Prophecies (Occultism)—History—Juvenile literature. [1. Prophets. 2. Prophecies—History.] I. Brooker, Kyrsten, ill.
II. Title.
BF1791.K78 1999
133.3—dc21
97-51705

FIRST
EDITION

Contents

For I dipp'd into the future,
as far as human eye could see,
Saw the vision of the world,
and all the wonder
that would be . . .
—*Alfred Lord Tennyson*

We offer our children courses in history;
why not also courses in
"Future" . . .
—*Alvin Toffler,* Future Shock

To Begin

Who hasn't wished to see the future?
And how would you feel if you really could?

Welcome to the world of people who have seen into the future. This volume collects, in chronological order, twelve such visionaries' stories, focusing on their rare talent to predict. These people were like lights in the darkness, wizards who lit up the harsh and sometimes ignorant lives of those around them. Just how did they *know*? And what do they have to say about the next century—the one with *you* in it?

Curiosity about the future is part of who we are. Universal emotions drive us: fear, helplessness, greed, grief, a desire for order, a sense of wonder that begs to be tickled. Those who see ahead satisfy for us deep emotional needs. They empower us by helping us to make choices. In turn, they become powerful figures—sometimes changing the course of history.

Especially during a fateful change, like the rolling of one century into another, "what's going to happen next?" can drive us crazy. The question is on everybody's minds, from heads of governments to those who play with Ouija boards at sleepovers. Millions of us seek out fortune-tellers, or flip first to their horoscope when reading a magazine or newspaper. Psychics are even accessible by phone. Profits from psychic hotlines are currently $1 *billion* a year—and predicted to keep soaring. At moments like this, moments of uncertainty, we desperately crave comfort. We want to know that what will happen to us is not random, out of the blue, out of our control.

Trying to get a grip on the future has motivated human behavior since the beginning of time. Prehistoric people hunted for omens in their dreams, the weather, the cries of birds, the sound of leaves rustling, the way the insides of animals looked when they were killed on altars.

The ancient Greeks refined these prehistoric notions into a system ruled by gods and goddesses. These divine beings made predictions through their human representatives: wise women known as *oracles*. The Oracle at Delphi influenced all aspects of society for an amazing one thousand years, while Greeks generated the ideas that formed the basis of Western civilization.

Those in ancient Rome paid attention to their legendary sibyls. The voices of these female prophets echoed from caves—sending mysterious reverberations throughout the Roman Empire.

The mighty Maya, believing in the power of the stars to tell our future, raised *astrology* to previously unheard-of heights.

Some of the individuals' names in this book are world-famous, such as awe-inspiring Nostradamus. This French doctor took on the task of predicting the entire history of the world. Others are lesser known, like Hildegard of Bingen. This German nun's uncanny insights were centuries ahead of her time.

Italian artist Leonardo da Vinci pursued a new kind of thinking called *science*. His fantastic inventions became reality—but only hundreds of years later.

Two people in this book combined science with stories. High-tech Jules Verne, in France, and the unnerving H. G. Wells, in England, co-created *science fiction*, a kind of seeing-into-the-future writing.

Nicholas Black Elk's intense observations of the American Indian's fate—formed into a cry for peace—were found prophetic decades later.

Jeane Dixon's predictions were notoriously outrageous. But during her prime, more people were listening to this American astrologer than to rulers of governments.

Few have ever equaled the accuracy of Edgar Cayce, the American visionary. Yet he insisted modestly that we can all be psychic—"The thoughts you hold create the currents over which the wings of your experience must go."

Marshall McLuhan, a nervous intellectual from Canada, never stopped asking the question, "What haven't you noticed lately?" Almost twenty years after his death, we can't get away from his farseeing answers.

Are there secrets to the success of these future-seers? Ultimately, an element of mystery thwarts us: Something about them—a gift, a talent, a special genius—will forever remain beyond rational explanation. We will never know exactly why these people, and not others, could perform such miraculous feats of the mind.

But it is fun to speculate. Most of these seers, for example, were outsiders, set apart from their times by major differences. Most became extremely well read, paying particular attention to history, science, and current events. Knowledge really *is* power, they found out. They tended to excel at listening. Their virtues included patience, tremendous curiosity, a sense of wonder, open-mindedness (without gullibility), and well-developed communication skills. They trained themselves to notice things the rest of us simply miss. From those who feared them as quacks or as satanic beings, they often faced ridicule, jail terms, and death threats, so they had to be strong personalities, willing to take risks. They knew others well but themselves even better. Solitude was a big help—many were almost recluses.

Something else helped these seers. Mixed in with all the science, writing, thinking, and paying attention was a lot of luck. In other words, some pretty good guessing. This book stars people whose documented speculations were more often right than wrong. But no one is perfect. Nostradamus had New York destroyed in a nuclear war. Verne thought we'd have mechanized dressing rooms that would wash and clothe us. Cayce saw California toppling into the ocean and a small town in Montana becoming the world's financial center. Dixon predicted a woman president of the United States by the 1980s. McLuhan was sure books would be obsolete by now.

Still, the idea of knowing the future is too delicious to ignore. Most of us overlook such wrong turns. For one prediction can't be argued with: People will continue to predict the future—and we will always be on the edge of our seats, thrilled to learn what they see.

The Oracle at Delphi

*"I know the number of the grains of sand,
and all the measures of the sea."*

A SERIES OF ALL-KNOWING
WOMEN IN ANCIENT GREECE WHO PROPHESIED
FROM ABOUT 700 B.C. TO A.D. 362

If you were a traveler in ancient Greece, you'd likely be heading to Delphi. The journey would be exhausting—weeks, even months, on dusty roads. Your personal safety would be at risk. During these chaotic times, threats range from attack by a brutal criminal all the way to ambush by an invading army. . . .

But you have heard so much about Delphi, the sacred center of the earth—its celebrated "navel." You have heard all about the remarkable women at a certain temple. You ache with curiosity about your future, and you know that Delphi is where you will find relief.

WHAT PILGRIMS SAW AT DELPHI

Coming around yet another bend in the endlessly curving road, you glimpse a new vista. The scenery is far more lush than anything on your journey thus far. A river winds its way through a valley, densely lined with silvery green olive trees. Your spirit lifts at the sight of the aqua water; the misty mountains in the background; the cypress, almond, and pine trees rustling in the cooling breeze. Twin limestone cliffs reflect the rays of the sun, flooding the area with light.

Dramatically flanked by the cliffs is the famed stone temple of Apollo, the god of light and truth. It literally glows from the sun. The columns around the temple are carved with solemn Greek wisdom: "Nothing in Excess" and "Know Thyself." Surrounding streets teem with thousands of priceless statues in bronze, marble, and gold.

You hurry to get into line with the other pilgrims. Pharaohs and kings and princes from distant lands have priority, then Greek citizens, then foreigners. Women, excluded from citizenship, are not allowed in line, but they have appointed men to represent them.

After paying your fee, you purify yourself with holy water and place a sacred cake on an altar as an offering. A priest approaches you and tells you to state a question.

The question can be personal: "What slave should I buy?" "Should I travel?" "Will the harvest be good?" "What is my child's destiny?" "Should I marry?" "What will the weather be?" "How can my illness be treated?" Or it can be political: "Should I go to war?" "What should my national policy be about religion?" "Should I make these laws?" You can ask for career advice, help in finding a missing person, a prediction about whether your wife or husband is going to be faithful, or a vision of which side will win a particular battle.

More priests take you underground, to a sanctuary constructed around the black stone believed to mark the exact center of the earth. The air is moist with vapors of a scent you can't identify. Before you towers a statue of Apollo flanked by two eagles, all of solid gold.

Nearby, behind a screen or curtain, is a mysterious woman known as the Pythia. Your human link to the god Apollo, she will obtain his answer to your question and share it with you. She wears formal robes and her forehead is bound by a wreath of laurel, Apollo's sacred plant. Priests burn barley meal and laurel leaves before her and give her more laurel to chew. She steps up to sit on a three-legged stool and begins breathing the vapors. The smell makes you dizzy.

The chief priest puts your question to the woman. Her face reddens. Suddenly she begins speaking, and her voice is strange . . . not of this earth. She talks in verse, which sometimes makes sense to you, sometimes not. Priests are on either side of her, listening intently, writing down what she says as fast as they can.

As the Pythia goes on with her riddles, her face empties of color. Her hair seems to stiffen and stand on end, and at one point she rips off her laurel wreath. Her legs and arms jerk, saliva appears at her lips, her eyes blaze.

Then she seems drained. So are you. Priests usher you back up into the daylight. They give you their translation of what the woman has spoken. You are confused, tired, but somehow content. You have what you wanted, what so many before you have sought at Delphi: a glimpse into the future, straight from a messenger of the divine Apollo himself.

DRAGON PRIESTESSES OF EARTH

The origins of Delphi's mysteries stretch far back into history. With their myths, the ancient Greeks had developed a complex system of gods and goddesses. Zeus was lord of the sky, and the most powerful of the gods. His son, Apollo, was the messenger between gods and humans. Getting a sign from a god came to be considered the most reliable way to know the future. Especially reliable were predictions at an oracle—a place where gods foretold the future through human representatives.

According to Greek myth, Zeus once sent out an eagle from the south and an eagle from the north. Where the two met would be marked the center of the earth. Greeks believed that spot to be Delphi, the loveliest landscape in Greece. At first it was a playground for goats, which thrived on its rocky, unstable terrain. Humans arrived to take care of them during the fourteenth century B.C.— that is, fourteen centuries before the birth of Christ.

One day a massive earthquake at Delphi created a large opening, or chasm, from which natural vapors, or gas, escaped. Goats began to act freakishly, going into spasms and bleating in a completely different voice. Goat keepers found themselves overcome by the vapors too. They began announcing weird things. Things that later came true.

Local peasants flocked to the site. At first, all was chaos: people went into trances all around the chasm, some even falling to their deaths. Around 700 B.C., locals decided to save lives by appointing one young woman as a sacred priestess. She would breathe the vapors and do the announcing. They built a three-legged stool so that she could sit over the opening without falling in.

The woman behaved and spoke as though possessed by something supernatural. People believed her words to be Apollo's. They gave her the title of the Pythia—Dragon Priestess of Earth—in honor of Python, the dragon-serpent that Apollo was said to have killed at the site. A vapor always enveloped the Pythia. Visitors described it sometimes as a marvelous perfume and sometimes as horribly sulfurous, supposedly coming from the body of the python rotting away in the chasm.

Over time, others took the place of the first Pythia. As a group, the women were known as the Oracle at Delphi. Other oracles existed, but Delphi was in a class by itself. Its influence spread throughout the world during centuries known as the golden age of Greece—and the birth of Western civilization. It was a stormy time when people craved what the oracle offered.

The Role of Women

It was an honor to be the Pythia. Women were believed to be more receptive to inspiration than men. At first locals picked young unmarried women, assuming them to be virgins with little knowledge of the world and most capable of accurately delivering the divine messages.

But young women were also the most vulnerable to sexual assault. Not long after the oracle was established at Delphi, a man from nearby Thessaly consulted the Pythia and then kidnapped and raped her. After this, the locals decided that a Pythia would be safer if she were over fifty years old—an aged woman in that day.

Because the women were regarded as unconscious instruments through which Apollo spoke, we don't know most of their real names. Chosen from the uneducated classes, they were presumed illiterate. Deep religious faith was a requirement, as were perfect behavior and good health. One test given to the prospective Pythia was to pour cold water over her to make sure she wasn't prone to hysteria that would muddle Apollo's signals. She could have a family of her own but had to live apart from her husband and wear the dress of a maiden (not a married woman). She wasn't supposed to talk about her work or even socialize. She fasted and purified herself daily, drinking and bathing in water piped in from a spring believed to be magic.

By the fifth century B.C., the height of Delphi's fame, two priestesses were kept constantly busy. A third was always prepared to take over in case one was ill or business was especially heavy. The work they did, entering trances several times a day, was clearly draining. Most Pythia, even though chosen for their sturdy nature, did not live long after taking on the job. At least once, a Pythia in a trance threw herself to the ground so violently that she died a few days later of her injuries.

THE ROLE OF MEN

The Pythia's trances were utterly mysterious. Any unlucky omen might put her into a bad mood, when she would speak in a gravelly voice or give terrifying shrieks. Some reports mention barking and other wild behavior; some describe an obscure, rambling style.

Her inscrutability didn't matter to the pilgrims. Male priests were always present to unravel her riddles and hand over a translation. The priests came from upper-class, highly educated families. They were not expected to have prophetic powers, like the Pythia, but to be shrewd and well informed.

Male historians have traditionally seen the priests as having the real power at Delphi. More recent views hold that the women were not as crazed as once thought and may indeed have been unusually wise.

Together these men and women fretted over their own safety. As the reputation of Delphi spread, they were vulnerable to threats of physical harm. Great care went into constructing predictions. Tact and quick thinking were especially crucial when addressing mighty rulers. The "wrong" answers might be met with a harsh, quite personal response—like instant death.

THE RESULTS

As it turned out, "wrong" answers were rare. Travelers hardly ever left disappointed.

King Croesus, ruler in the 600s B.C. of what is now part of Turkey, started out as a skeptic. To Delphi and some six other oracles of the day, he sent messengers with this question: "What will the King be doing in his palace one hundred days after his messengers leave?" On that day, he secretly cut up a lamb and a tortoise, and cooked them together in a bronze pot, covering it so no one could look inside. It was the most unlikely, bizarre thing he could think of to do.

Of all the replies he got, only the Pythia was unfazed: "I know the number of the grains of sand, and all the measures of the sea," she responded. "I understand the dumb, and the speechless I hear. The smell has come to my nostrils of a hard-skinned tortoise as it is boiled with lamb's flesh in a covered vessel, all of bronze."

Astounded, King Croesus forever after considered Delphi a virtual guarantee of accuracy. He set the trend in sending gifts of gratitude. Besides ordering the sacrifice of three hundred animals to Apollo, he delivered his own purple tunics, robes of pearl, a gold bowl large enough to hold five thousand gallons of wine, and a solid gold statue of the woman who cooked his pastries.

Sometime later he asked if his son, unable to speak since birth, would ever

talk. The Pythia replied: "Desire not to hear within your halls the voice long prayed for of your son speaking . . . For he will speak first on a day of ill fortune." Soon the king was under attack by a rival nation. When the army broke into the palace and rushed to kill the royal family, the son cried out his first words: "Wretch, would you slay Croesus?"

The Pythia's replies could be unrelated to the question asked of her. When a Greek named Battus sought help for his stutter, the Pythia replied that he would establish a city in North Africa. Battus later founded the city of Cyrene in Libya—still stuttering.

In time no one dared sail forth to claim other lands without a nod of approval from Delphi. One colonizer was told that when rain fell on him from a clear sky he was to seize a certain city. The sky remained cloudless, yet no rain fell, and he made no headway. Depressed, he went to Aethra, his wife, for solace. He laid his head on her lap, and she felt so sorry for him that she began to weep as she deloused his hair. Finally he understood: *Aethra* meant "clear sky," and her tears were falling on his face. The next night he attacked the city and captured it.

You could petition a Pythia twice if you were unhappy the first time. The Athenians did this when, fearing their city was about to be attacked, they got this warning: "Hence from my temple! Bow your hearts to doom!"

They petitioned again, asking for a future less cruel. She gave an answer just as obscure but slightly more hopeful. Unfortunately, a terrific battle ensued, and enemies set Athens on fire. Still, when the surviving Athenians emerged to survey their ruined city, they were encouraged: Their sacred olive tree was alive and sending up fresh green shoots.

Sometimes a petition was unnecessary. This was proved by Alexander the Great, whose role in history was to spread the new ideas of Greek civilization throughout the known world. Arriving in Delphi, he refused to accept it when told that the Pythia refused to prophecy that day. Enraged, he raced to her home and tried to drag her forcibly to the temple.

"You are invincible, my son," the Pythia said, impressed at his authority. That was actually all he wanted to hear, and he took off without an official consultation.

The thirty-year-old Roman emperor Nero, after assassinating his mother, had mixed feelings about the message he got: "Your presence outrages me. Begone, matricide! Beware of seventy-three!" The good news, he thought, was that he would live another forty-three years. But he was furious at being called a mother murderer. He ordered the hands and feet of the priestess and priests cut off, then had them buried alive. He helped himself to five hundred of Delphi's statues and moved them to Rome. He died only a year later—the prophecy apparently referred to Galba, his seventy-three-year-old successor.

Eventually, just about anyone who doubted Delphi ended up a believer.

Skeptical Greek philosophers who questioned *everything* trusted Delphi—especially Socrates, the famous intellectual from Athens, whom the oracle had named "the wisest of men."

Streams of grateful travelers left gifts for Apollo. Lavish stone storehouses were built to protect the jewels, paintings, fabrics, and other treasures.

Cicero, the Roman philosopher, wrote: "Never could the Oracle at Delphi have been so overwhelmed with so many important offerings from monarchs and nations if all the ages had not proved the truth of its oracles."

WHAT WAS DELPHI'S SECRET?

One technique favored by the oracle was vagueness. Sometimes the Pythia's words could be interpreted in completely opposite ways. As one observer said, the oracle "neither reveals or conceals, but hints." These were statements about the will of the gods that *you* had to interpret. The ambiguity forced you inward for a key—but it also meant that the oracle was always right. The Pythia never apologized. Any disasters were due to misinterpretation—your own fault.

What accounted for the Pythia's trances? Natural gases from earthquake chasms aren't generally hallucinogenic. Perhaps parts of the ritual helped to induce a state of self-hypnosis. Perhaps it was the laurel, which throughout history has been used for various medicinal purposes.

The biggest clue to the oracle's success is, simply, information. The area quickly became a magnet for current news. Coming into contact with so many strangers each day, the priests and priestesses gained insights that others didn't. They learned so much about geography, for example, that they knew which areas had yet to be colonized—and sent Greeks there to claim them.

In numerous cases, however, there are simply no rational explanations for the oracle's accuracy. For this powerful reason, its influence prevailed for almost a thousand years. With predictions so wide-ranging, both personal and political, the oracle affected everyone in some way or another, often to a considerable extent. Its prophecies profoundly influenced the ruling of empires, as well as day-to-day living. For those too poor to afford the fee, a Pythia would sit on the temple steps once a year and reply to problems brought to her.

Very slowly, doubts about the Pythia's integrity grew. Was she deducing, perhaps from the way pilgrims worded their questions, what the asker's intentions were or what answers they expected? Rival countries looted Delphi's treasures. Astrology, or predictions based on movements of the stars, became all the rage. Then came science, a more systematic way of thinking: viewing the world as ruled by the laws of nature, not by gods. Christianity, a new religion, banned oracle prophesying as pagan rites.

The last recorded prophecy was in A.D. 362, or 362 years after the birth of Christ. It was for Julian, the last Roman emperor to oppose Christianity. In it the Pythia predicted her own demise: "The voice is stilled." Earthquakes, fires, landslides, and wars took their toll. A whole new town, Kastri, was built on top of the ruins of Delphi, truly stilling the oracle's voice.

LASTING EFFECTS

The oracle's popularity corresponded with a cultural surge unequaled in world history. Delphi was the source of guidance as Greeks developed new kinds of literature, art, science, mathematics, and philosophy—ideas that ended up being the foundation of Western civilization. The laws for a new form of government known as democracy were approved at Delphi.

As the highest spiritual authority of its time, the oracle is believed to have changed behavior. Historians have called it "the conscience of Greece." For example, in recommending that meals be cooked and eaten in common, the oracle sought to abolish illness due to gluttony. The prophecies urged moderation in all things, generally good manners—respect for the lives of women and slaves, religious tolerance, the value of keeping one's word. They consistently promoted compassion for the handicapped and warned against using superstition as an excuse for cruelty. Over the dark chaos of ignorance, the oracle forged patterns based on law and order.

Hundreds of years after the oracle's voice was silenced, French archaeologists arrived to excavate the site's remains. In the 1890s, Kastri was moved elsewhere, and the oracle began revealing itself to the modern world.

Today Delphi is still a mystical shrine for pilgrims. Hearts still stop at the gorgeous scenery. And tourists still seek out the ruins of the temple—for answers to their own questions perhaps, and to marvel at the dazzling power that women here once wielded.

The Sibyls

"I am born betwixt a mortal and a god . . ."

THESE MYSTERIOUS WOMEN OF
THE ROMAN EMPIRE WERE POWERFUL
FROM AROUND 1200 B.C. UNTIL
AFTER THE BIRTH OF CHRIST

Across from Greece, also on the Mediterranean Sea, another civilization mushrooms: the mighty Roman Empire. Thanks to its ingenious system of new roads, communication has become easier than it's ever been. The empire rapidly outgrows Italy and conquers what will become parts of Africa, Asia, the Middle East, and all of southern Europe. One fifth of all the people in the world must obey Roman laws and pay taxes to the emperor. All roads now truly lead to Rome, the new center of the world, a chaotic city of almost a million.

But for all the Roman Empire's glorious achievements, it is a bloodthirsty, cruel society, based on force and violence. Hundreds of amphitheaters all over the empire feature gladiators who fight each other to the death in enormously popular spectacles of gore. Watching them somehow relieves the pressures of daily life, which overwhelm its citizens with a crushing burden of decisions to make and much personal danger. Everyone struggles to conform to the laws of the emperor, but there's a new one so often—up to four a year and not all of them sane or fair. If you're a male property owner, required to serve sixteen long years in the all-powerful Roman army, you must protect your family and home during your absence. If you're a woman, you have no rights and are vulnerable at all times. Slaves, who at times outnumber the citizens, are disposable property that owners can sell, torture, or kill for any reason.

Perilous natural disasters threaten everyone, as do unbearably high taxes. All are nervous about religious ceremonies—which ones should be performed to appease the Roman gods, rather than anger them?

Luckily, in a citizen's search for stability, there is help: You have the predictions made by women known as sibyls.

True, no one has ever seen a sibyl with his own eyes. But everyone knows what she is like. At least they *think* they know.

A sibyl gets her eerie visions after drinking bull's blood, a deadly poison . . . to everyone except a sibyl. She speaks in an odd, bat-like voice. It's been reported that she is at least 110 years old, maybe centuries older. As she ages, she is said to shrink. Some say she can even fit into a flask—none of her visible, just a voice.

Above all, she is wise, and her wisdom enables others to plan ahead.

NEIGHBORHOOD WISE WOMEN

At some point before 1200 B.C., the local wisewoman, or healer, was known by her real name. But as she took on a more influential role in the community—gaining respect for her second sight, the ability to see into the future—people began to use "Sibyl" as her title. In the mist of centuries past, perhaps one particularly astute woman actually was named Sibyl. But, over time, all female psychics came to be called sibyls.

The sibyls grew into a long line of learned priestesses, venerated for centuries throughout the Mediterranean world. The earliest reference to one, around 1200 B.C., is from what is now Turkey. She claimed to be half divine: "I am born betwixt a mortal and a god, of an immortal nymph and a father feeding on bread." This sibyl not only foretold the upcoming Trojan War but also predicted that the Greek poet Homer would borrow her verses for his epic poems about it, the *Iliad* and the *Odyssey*.

Sibyls had little in common with typical women of their day. A Roman girl went straight from her father's authority to her husband's. Her role was to have children, take care of the house, and no more. But the sibyls lived independently and their singular talent of second sight made them exotic and eccentric. They earned money and were free to cultivate their awareness of the world around them. Like all Roman females, they had not been permitted to attend school as children, but they must have somehow educated each other. Presumably they passed the body of their mystical knowledge from priestess to priestess, perhaps during ceremonies so secret they have never come to light.

THE ROLE OF SIBYLS

Sibyls seem to have been to Rome what the Oracle at Delphi was to Greece, with certain differences. One is that little scholarly research has been devoted to sibyls. The text of their predictions is almost entirely lost, often deliberately destroyed by unbelievers who came later. With evidence about them so limited, only guesswork can fill in details.

We know that while the oracle answered specific questions asked by individuals, the sibyls offered more general forecasts for the enlightenment of whoever heard them. They addressed events of broad significance, frequently focusing on doom and destruction.

A sibyl once foretold a series of earthquakes, for example. Whole cities would slide, and the "greatest evil" would come to a certain island near Turkey. This island, Rhodes, was in fact notorious for exactly that kind of disaster.

Thus, the prediction's accuracy was likely. Sibyls excelled at these artfully vague descriptions of past and current events, shaped into prophecies.

A sibyl's words were not particularly poetic, but they served the most useful of functions: they comforted people. They showed that disasters were not random, but part of a pattern that could be predicted. The Romans had a wide variety of religious beliefs in addition to sibylline predictions. But just as the Oracle at Delphi steadied people during a time of intense growth, so the sibyls raised morale during turmoil.

Unlike the oracle, a sibyl kept her own personality: when she said "I" she referred to herself. (Delphi, on the other hand, was completely possessed by Apollo: when the Pythia said "I" she meant the god himself was speaking.)

The women at Delphi were at least fifty, but sibyls were even older. A sibyl could claim to have foretold events—such as an invasion or a severe drought—that people would recognize as parts of their past. Then, shifting to talk of the future, she would sound infallible. She had already been proven correct with the events she had lived through.

Sibyls showed up everywhere in folklore and art of this time. From the great Roman poet Virgil on, writers made so much of these unearthly women that it was clearly safe to assume the reading public knew them well. This familiar figure sometimes appeared in ways not meant to be taken literally. Somehow the legend arose that her life span was 1,000 years, or at the very least 110. Virgil regularly cracked jokes about "the long-lived priestess" and the way she could shrink. Writers chuckled about stone jars containing a sibyl—her cremated body, or her shrunken bones, or simply a voice. The Greek philosopher Heracleitus, for example, described the way "Sibylla, with raving mouth uttering things without laughter and without charm of sight or scent, reaches a thousand years by her voice."

While the Oracle at Delphi only *spoke* her verses, a sibyl was educated enough to put hers in writing. Versions of sibylline prophecies circulated widely among all classes of people, and any crisis sparked renewed attention to them.

THE SIBYL AND THE KING

Historians have identified at least ten sibyls. The most famous, and the only one for whom archaeological evidence exists, was the Cumaean sibyl. Over the centuries, a series of women took on the role of a sibyl in Cumae (now Cuma) on the Bay of Naples. This was the earliest colony on the Italian mainland and it eventually became a major harbor, the refueling site for all voyages in the area.

This sibyl's business office was a cave, high on a red volcanic hill, overlooking the sea. The Greek poet Lycophron wrote of "the priestess-maid" in her "awful dwelling-place, a yawning cavern roofed with arching rocks." The cave was trapezoidal, a shape now known to be more earthquake resistant. Windows cut through the rock lit the space diagonally. It was clean and well ventilated, with smooth walls. In the passageway, parallel to the cliff, were six openings. Echoes of the sibyl's voice would have reverberated eerily. Poets interpreted the openings as the means by which her wisdom reached the outside world. Virgil exaggerated the six openings into a hundred: "a hundred mouths from which as many voices pour."

After bathing and purifying herself, she was said to have dressed in long ceremonial robes, gone to her chamber, and sat on a throne. Her inspiration was believed to have come from this ritual bath or from the act of entering Mother Earth by way of the cave.

Her predictions were in Greek, Hebrew, Latin, or hieroglyphics. She spoke them, or wrote them, sometimes in bizarre signs and symbols. She loved to play word games, indicating that she prophesied with careful thought, not in a frenzy. She could be evasive and even teasing. Sometimes she wrote on palm leaves that the winds blew about, much to people's consternation.

The most famous story about the Cumaean sibyl begins with the day, around 525 B.C., that she appeared in Rome. The strange old woman asked to see King Tarquin. She offered to sell him her nine books containing the destiny of the world.

She was so aged that the king treated her as senile. He thought her price of three hundred pieces of gold was crazy and sent her away, making fun of her. Some time later she returned and offered to sell him six books for the same price. Again he sent her away. Finally she appeared with three books, again for the same price. Impressed with her persistence, and starting to believe that something serious was at stake, Tarquin paid her fee. After looking them over, he demanded the other six books. She said she had burned them—then she disappeared and was never seen again.

A whole college of priests was hurriedly assigned to reconstitute the other six books, as best they could from guesswork and second-hand reports. For centuries afterward, according to legend, Rome was cursed to *never know its future.*

With life in the city so lawless, Tarquin fretted over how to protect the large collections of predictions. He decided that the only safe place was a stone chest underneath the temple of Jupiter, on the Capitoline Hill. The *Sibylline Books* became the most heavily guarded possessions in Rome. The senate decreed that they were to be consulted only in emergencies and before any great decision. Even the high priests couldn't look at them without a special order from the senate. Anyone else who tried was sewn into a sack and thrown into the river.

THE END OF THE WORLD

Like the Oracle at Delphi, the *Sibylline Books* emphasized that the secret to a happy life was to "know thyself." Natural disasters would come in threes, they predicted. A comet was an early warning sign of a war. A tree that sank into the ground, with only a few branches showing, was a warning about forthcoming human slaughter.

To increase harvests and check famine, the books recommended an annual fast in honor of Ceres, goddess of the growth of food plants. (Perhaps the books were trying to replace a more cruel ceremony that honored Ceres: tying torches to the tails of foxes and setting them loose inside stadiums.) To get rid of the deadly plague, they prescribed a new ritual called a *lestisternium:* statues of six gods and goddesses were grouped in pairs on three couches, with feasts laid before them. "All forums and marketplaces" around the empire, not just the city of Rome, were to partake in ceremonies like this, the books advised.

Some three hundred years after the *Sibylline Books* were reconstructed, they were still giving guidance. During Hannibal's invasion of Italy in 204 B.C., Romans interpreted the books as telling them to fetch from Asia a certain black stone. Belonging to the "Mother" of the gods—the "Giver of Life"—this stone would protect the Romans, who later did succeed in turning back Hannibal.

The Cumaean sibyl foretold the end of the world in a way that sounds like the script for a contemporary horror film: "Then shall the elements of all the world be desolate; air, earth, sea, flaming fire, and the sky and night, all days merge into one fire, and to one barren, shapeless mass to come." The death of humanity would soon follow: "A single day will see the burial of mankind, all that the long forbearance of fortune has produced, all that has been raised to eminence, all that is famous and all that is beautiful; great thrones, great nations—all will descend into one abyss, all will be overthrown in one hour."

Indeed, the world in which the sibyls were powerful *was* ending. In the coming centuries, Italy was overtaken by invaders. The glory of the Roman Empire faded. In 83 B.C., the precious *Sibylline Books* burned in a fire that also destroyed the temple. Emperors began substituting astrology for sibylline prophecy, commanding people to look to the movements of the stars for predictions. Later rulers banned astrology and imposed upon the Roman Empire a brand-new system of beliefs called Christianity. The first Christians honored the Cumaean sibyl because it was rumored she had foretold the birth of Christ. But soon Christianity put an end to all rites and beliefs considered pagan, or opposed to the one true God. The sibyls fell into this category. The centuries of their immense power were over.

As for the Cumaean sibyl, her cave was eventually filled in by earthquakes. Thousands of years later, in 1932, archaeologists arrived. They excavated a system of caverns that corresponded to accounts about her. They discovered an ancient tunnel, nearly five hundred feet long, that had been drilled through solid rock—an engineering feat requiring a tremendous labor force. The sibyl must have been something like a public institution. Even the coins found in the area were engraved with her symbol, a mussel shell.

MOMENT OF TRIUMPH ON THE CEILING

Early Christians didn't abandon sibyls all at once. At first, they used sibyls as universally recognized figures they could discredit and then replace with new ideas. A Christian writer would take a sibyl's forecast of doom, for example, and give it a twist: Only members of the new religion would survive the predicted disaster and live on in the kingdom of God.

Later Christians made a point of destroying any remaining evidence of the pagan priestesses. Over the course of the next thousand years, the sibyls passed into myth as figures of fantasy.

In 1512, the great Italian painter Michelangelo completed the vaulted ceiling of the Sistine Chapel in Rome. Everyone wondered: Who were these five striking women painted in company with seven of the Old Testament prophets?

They were sibyls, and Michelangelo's painting—done at a time when women scholars were nonexistent—renewed interest in these learned women. As was his habit, Michelangelo used males as models for the women's bodies. The sibyls he depicted look very strong—strong enough to carry the nine huge *Sibylline Books*. The effect of this famous ceiling was to improve the reputation of these women; sibyls came to seem less pagan and more acceptable to a Christian society.

If only a sibyl were still alive today to answer our many questions about the priestesses and their prophecies. One thing is clear though: After the sibyls' prominence, women's wisdom went underground and was not heard in public for hundreds of years.

The Maya

"As above, so below."

AT THEIR HEIGHT BETWEEN
A.D. 250 AND 900, THE MAYAN PEOPLE
OF MEXICO AND CENTRAL AMERICA
FOCUSED INTENSELY ON ASTROLOGY AS
A WAY TO CONTROL THE FUTURE

Screaming monkeys jump from trees. Wild jaguars stalk human prey. Poisonous snakes slither about, unnoticed.

For any Maya, survival is chancy, living in a jungle that is simply not hospitable to human life.

Still, nothing is more spectacular to the Maya than the birth of a child. As soon as you're born, your mother washes you; then, if you're of noble birth, she fastens you to a cradle that compresses your head between boards. After two days your head is permanently flattened—a mark of great beauty. She might also hang a small bead in the hair over your nose, to make your eyes cross, another trait held in high esteem among the noble class.

Then—whether noble, peasant, or slave—your parents take you to the priest as soon as possible. From this man they will learn your destiny: whether you will be a warrior or a tattoo artist, a murderer or a thief. Or perhaps it is your fate to be sacrificed. . . .

THE KEY TO SURVIVAL

A tropical rain forest envelops most of the Mayan territory, in which ferocious animals and even more ferocious insects breed. In some areas the soil is deep and fertile; in others it is bone-dry unless the rainy season has turned it into a swamp. Diseases spread rapidly. Yet there are millions of Maya—fourteen million at the civilization's height.

How can you survive, to help grow the beans, chile peppers, and squash that will keep everyone fed? And especially the corn, the basis for every single meal in tortillas, gruels, even drinks. The god of corn is more important than any in the complex Mayan pantheon—more exalted than the sun god, the moon god, the rain god, and all the other representatives of nature.

You must know your destiny, to learn what role you will play in a society that depends on agriculture. And you must be able to foretell the weather, to grasp some measure of control over the food supply. You must try to order the chaos that surrounds you.

Fortunately, there are priests who specialize in what you need: predictions. Such a priest is called by a title meaning "he who knows," or "interpreter of the gods." Honored by all, he is carried around on other people's shoulders. Wearing many jewels and feathers, he gathers listeners together and reads aloud from the sacred books. Sometimes he reports on visions he receives after partaking of tobacco mixed with lime, peyote, or hallucinogenic mushrooms. Sometimes he sings his predictions or acts them out to the accompaniment of drums.

Your need to see the future motivates your life, and priests are your key to survival.

IN LOVE WITH NUMBERS

The Mayan people of Mexico and Central America are generally regarded as the greatest ancient civilization of the New World. They triumphed over thousands of years, reaching their peak of creativity between A.D. 250 and 900. And they continue to baffle us. By what clever farming techniques did they support themselves for so long? How did they come by their amazing achievements in math, including the use of zero? (Try to imagine math without it.) Without modern instruments, such as telescopes, how did they master astronomy? How did they pepper their jungle with forty monumental cities full of pyramid temples twenty-two stories high?

And how did they predict the future—an accomplishment that may have enabled their civilization to thrive against tremendous odds?

Some of these questions can be addressed by looking at the Mayan obsession with counting and measuring. More than any culture in history, they worshiped time, numbers, and astrology. Their form of future-predicting was based on the theory that human affairs are guided by the movements of the stars, planets, sun, and moon. Plenty of people, including some contemporary Americans, find astrology compelling. But the Maya actually organized their entire society around it, trying to make sense of the great unknown above them.

Your birth date *was* your fate. It was believed to determine how you would interact with other people and the world. If you were born on the date that the Mayan calendar specified for farmer, beekeeper, tattoo artist, singer, poet, dancer, murderer, or thief . . . that's what you would be. Males born on days known as Chuen or Kan would become craftsmen, for example. Those born on Cib or Hix would be warriors, and those born on Edznab were destined to be doctors. (Women played far fewer roles in Mayan life.)

Your parents' role was to guide your upbringing according to this fate. And your role, as a Mayan child, was to submit to the power of the universe. You wanted to go with the current of the cosmos, not against it.

"HE WHO KNOWS"

Priests not only supervised the rituals and ceremonies of the Mayan religion; they were also astronomers—a measure of how important the stars were to this society. Astronomer-priests obsessively observed the skies. In this time before telescopes, they used their buildings to track particular stars, the sun, and the moon. Observatories comprised a maze of narrow tunnels and steep stairways, all constructed to align at certain angles so that windows would reveal different regions of the sky. Not having electric lights to muddy the view was an advantage. Generation after generation, priests compared notes to gather remarkably precise data and detect patterns for forecasting weather.

Over thousands of years, the priests carved their sacred calculations on temples and upright stone monuments. They also wrote books, with paper made from the inner bark of wild fig trees and covers made from jaguar skin. Using a system of writing called hieroglyphics—so complex that archaeologists couldn't decipher it until the mid-twentieth century—the books recorded events and made predictions, based on astronomy.

"As above, so below," was a Mayan saying—that is, truth was in the skies. The priests weren't just talking about weather, but about forecasting future human events. An example of a prophecy is the one for Katun 13 Ahau, a date that occurs every 260 Mayan years:

> *On that day, dust possess the earth,*
> *On that day, a blight is on the face of the earth.*
> *On that day, a cloud rises,*
> *On that day, a mountain rises,*
> *On that day, a strong man seizes the land,*
> *On that day, things fall to ruin,*
> *On that day, the tender leaf is destroyed,*
> *On that day, the dying eyes are closed.*

As this date approached (the next Katun 13 Ahau occurs on May 30, 2052), priests would interpret the meaning of the warnings according to current events. They might specify what "strong man" was likeliest to cause trouble, or what day a terrible dust storm might happen.

They would also interpret happenings of the past as indicating omens of the future. People who neglected history were apt to repeat it. A ruler who forgot, for instance, that certain actions once caused a war with a rival city was doomed to cause another war.

In order to survive a disaster forecasted by the priests, no effort was too costly. Torture and human sacrifice were Mayan rituals believed to keep their gods happy. Illegitimate children or orphans, with no parents to protect them, were vulnerable to being sacrificed, as were defeated rulers, prisoners of war, and criminals. Victims could be abducted or bought, and the going price was five to ten stone beads per child. Mayans also tried less brutal ways to change fate, like fasting, dancing, and offerings of prayer, food, animals, jewels, and incense.

Being a priest was a hereditary office, and all priests went to special schools to learn their duties. Some supervised sacrifices, with responsibilities like splitting open victims' breasts, or holding down arms and legs. Some treated disease, healing with herbs as well as potions of bat wings, animal excrement, blood, crocodile testicles, bird fat, and red worms. But none were more revered than those who specialized in interpreting predictions.

THE AMAZING SACRED CALENDAR

Invented by priests approximately 2,600 years ago, the Mayan calendar is considered by some scholars to be the most accurate ever devised. According to the Maya's highly sophisticated calculations, the world had a definite beginning: a date known as 4 Ahau 8 Cumku, or August 13, 3114 B.C.

The calendar was made up of at least two complex, interlocking cycles running at the same time. The first was a 365-day cycle, known as Tun, divided into eighteen months of twenty days each. The five days left over were considered extremely unlucky, requiring many sacrificial rituals. The second cycle, known as Tzolkin, was made up of thirteen months of twenty days apiece. Every single day had its own omens, prophecies, and associations—good, bad, and neutral. Exactly how the Maya determined these details is not known.

But if you wanted to plant corn, get married, or build a house, you tried to choose good days or, at least, neutral ones. Those making journeys—say merchants on shopping trips or warriors attacking rival Mayan cities—waited until lucky days to depart.

The calendar also dictated the intervals at which human blood was to be drawn. Rulers had to undergo ritual self-torture, such as drawing blood. They drew a thorn-studded cord through their tongues or jabbed needles or stingray spines through various body parts. Spattered on paper or collected in other ways, human blood was thought to nourish the gods.

Even more alarming, the Mayan calendar appears to have a final date for the world. And it's in our lifetime: the winter solstice (December 21) of 2012. Currently we are living in the last twenty-year period (or Katun), also known as the Maya's Fifth Creation Epoch. In the fateful year of 2012, three cycles in the Mayan calendar will end at the same time: the Katun, the current Baktun (twenty Katuns), and the current Creation Epoch (thirteen Baktuns, or a little less than 5,200 years). This conspicuous coincidence is supposed to mark the world's end. Humans will be punished with earthquakes, volcanoes, hurricanes, and tidal waves for the pain they've inflicted on the earth. Technology will become our enemy, and pets we have caged will turn on us.

Not all scholars of Mayan studies agree on this interpretation. Some feel the ancient Mayans meant that 2012 would introduce destruction merely as a way to cleanse the earth. Perhaps a new world would be created to let the cycles go on. The pace of research on the Maya is very rapid, and recent interpretations show their calendar not ending in 2012 at all. Some actually show it advancing into the fiftieth century.

WHERE DID THEY GO?

Among the many Mayan mysteries, the biggest is the disappearance of their whole civilization. Sometime around A.D. 900, there may have been widespread warfare. Severe drought, overpopulation and overcultivation of the soil may have led to famine. Whatever the reason, the Maya stopped building things and observing the skies. They took their books of predictions and dispersed into the surrounding wilderness. Jungle growth took over their cities.

The arrival of explorers from Spain meant that most Mayan people who could be found were doomed. The Spanish assumed the Mayans were mere corn-growing peasants, savages who probably couldn't count to ten on their fingers. The explorers made a point of destroying evidence of Mayan culture, like the precious books of prophecies. One Spanish priest wrote in 1562: "We found a great number of books [twenty-seven, to be exact]. . . and because they contained nothing but superstition and the devil's falsehoods, we burned the lot, which upset them most grievously and caused them great pain."

Thus thousands of years' worth of ancient astronomical research disappeared. Today we have only four fragments of the once enormous body of prophecies. This explains the frustrating lack of details concerning specific predictions.

Despite all this, the Mayan population did not die out. Several million of their descendants still live in what today is southern Mexico (Chiapas), as well as areas of Central America including El Salvador, northern Guatemala, and northern Belize. Even though the Maya remain under attack on all sides—from tourism, destruction of the rain forests, and corrupt military regimes trying to crush them—Mayan people are multiplying, not diminishing.

Mayan ideas, especially about prophecy and the nature of time, have lived on to form core beliefs for many American Indian tribes. Mayan society has intrigued thousands of contemporary scholars, who have dedicated their lives, and millions of dollars, to unearthing remnants of its richly ornamented cities.

And in the more isolated areas, Mayan astronomer-priests still consult with anxious parents and still keep track of the days by way of the sacred calendar.

Hildegard of Bingen

"I see and hear and understand at one and the same time."

A GERMAN NUN (1098–1179)
OF THE MIDDLE AGES, FILLED
WITH VISIONARY IDEAS
800 YEARS AHEAD OF HER TIME

What could you do if you were a young girl who had visions, made predictions, displayed an extraordinary range of talents, and knew about faraway places or scenes from the past?

In Germany during the Middle Ages, such a girl had few options. The Middle Ages, from roughly the fifth to the fifteenth centuries, did not tolerate oddballs. Christianity had unified all aspects of European culture. Church officials—men, all—controlled society, and their focus was the worship of God and the salvation of souls. Developments in science, the arts, education—none of which was considered Church business—came to a virtual stop. In medicine, for example, European knowledge lagged far behind that in Asian and Arab countries.

Wisewomen no longer commanded the respect of their communities. Superstition and stereotypes restricted the behavior of all women. Females were believed to be passive and less intelligent than males, and no respectable profession was open to them. Those who displayed something as startling as psychic gifts suffered death or persecution. Surely they were witches—under Satan's power. A slightly better fate was to be labeled crazy and be locked away.

Only in the convent was some honor possible.

WALLED OFF FROM THE WORLD

Hildegard was born in 1098 to a noble German family; her father was a knight. Three years later she began having visions. "But because I was an infant I could reveal nothing of it," she later wrote.

Once she could express herself properly, people found her unnerving. She seemed to know things before they happened. She once told, for example, what color a calf would be, before it was born.

When she turned eight, her parents dedicated her to the Catholic Church and delivered her to a convent to be educated. She grew up inside a small room with only one window, through which she received food. She spent her time in prayer and in silence, fasting, embroidering, and studying. In her teens she became a nun in the Benedictine order. These nuns followed the rules of Saint Benedict, who stressed work and study rather than a life of prayer only. Hildegard convinced others of her leadership qualities, as well as her talent for healing and prophecy. At age thirty-eight, she was unanimously elected head of her convent.

Later she moved to Bingen, on the banks of the Rhine River, where she administered a convent and a monastery, with a hundred people under her care. Convent life gave her financial independence, freedom from a domestic and reproductive role, and support as she thrived.

A LIGHT IN THE DARKNESS

A remarkable person by any standards, Hildegard was definitely ahead of her own time, an inspirational "first" in many fields.

In her day, sick people usually called priests to their bedsides, not doctors. Mixing superstition with ignorance, doctors usually made things worse. They had no concept of how disease spread, didn't isolate sick people from others, and knew nothing about the danger of unsanitary practices like letting garbage pile up in the streets until rain washed it away. The state of women's medicine was particularly bleak. Wanting to concentrate on the "worthier" sex, most doctors wouldn't even treat women; and childbirth was frequently fatal.

Hildegard was a healer with a quality of observation unique among her peers. Familiar with the crude science of her day, she took it further. She became an expert herbalist, collecting into books over 2,000 remedies. In these books, she talked about the circulatory system three centuries before it was "discovered." One of the first Europeans to mention a powerful body-mind-spirit connection, she wrote texts on holistic healing. She was also one of the world's first environmentalists, and wrote books about the sacred relationship between humans and the natural world.

Hildegard also became the first specialist in women's medicine. She believed women should take care of themselves with hot mineral baths, exercise, rest, and "radiating" (dressing in rich fabrics of warm colors).

Indeed, Hildegard was one of the world's first feminists—as much as the Middle Ages permitted. She showed no shyness about promoting herself and her work, traveled hundreds of miles, and had male secretaries. During years when men had a monopoly on the written word, she produced major works of theology. Upon request, she gave written advice to four popes, two emperors, at least one king, and several saints. She preached sermons to men, something considered impossible for a woman. When called upon to perform an exorcism of the devil—also unheard of for a woman to do—she carried out the ceremony capably, and made sure she had seven priests present to witness it. Considering herself a female warrior, she fought to shed light on the corruption of the Church's patriarchal hierarchy.

Hildegard is also the first composer whose biography is known. She wrote the first opera, as well as brilliant chants for women singers. Music was to her the highest form of activity—something that could restore the earth's balance. (She believed that Satan had no rhythm and lived in a place of "no-music.")

In her spare time, she invented "Lingua Ignola," or Unknown Language. Its alternative alphabet of letters and its nine hundred nouns were possibly a secret language the nuns used when they didn't want outsiders to understand them.

THE LIVING LIGHT

Hildegard got her ideas from the visions that continued to haunt her. She saw ways to treat medical conditions, solutions to scientific and theological problems, guidelines for human conduct, and images of an ideal future where women were honored.

During her visions, her eyes remained open and she was conscious. "I see and hear and understand at one and the same time," she reported. She painted what she saw, showing herself as a tiny seated figure with an open book, gazing upward at huge angels and demons, swirling winds and stars, even mixed-up creatures like a three-winged being with a fiery red human face.

She interpreted in a religious way the symbols that came to her, but from a unique perspective. She saw the universe, for example, as a cosmic egg in which God, people, and nature were connected. She saw dazzling, powerful female figures as "brilliant as the sun," with the creativity to "enkindle the moon, enliven the waters, and awaken everything to life." Some were goddesses from ancient cultures, and figures from the Bible. And some were God, whom Hildegard saw as partly female. Turning public opinion on its head, she believed that women were more, not less, spiritual than men. Her visions were a way to explain to herself her own power—the way she could see beyond a society that perpetually demeaned women.

Hildegard often mentioned a radiant light, inside of which was an even brighter light that she called "the living light." Light was the source of her knowledge, and she described herself as giving answers "from the blaze of the living light."

Not everyone could have tolerated her experiences. "From the very day of her birth," she wrote of herself, "this woman has lived with painful illnesses as if caught in a net, so that she is constantly tormented by pain in her veins, marrow and flesh." But the light made her lose all anxiety, as well as her sense of self: "I do not know myself, either in body or soul. And I consider myself as nothing."

At first she was embarrassed—what she saw was so confusing and inconvenient—and kept the visions to herself. But when she fell seriously ill in her late forties, she felt it was the result of this secretiveness. After consulting with the pope, she published the first of her collections of visions. In *Scivias* (or *Know the Ways* or *May You Know*), she shaped her visions into instructions on how to live. She believed, for example, that God put life into plants, animals, and precious gems. By eating the right foods and acquiring some of the gems, humans could lead more virtuous lives.

"SIBYL OF THE RHINE"

Eventually, Hildegard was pursued for advice, comfort, and assistance. From popes to commoners, all levels of society in Germany and abroad trusted her. People reverently called her a saint, though the Church never formally canonized her as one.

She also became known as "Sibyl of the Rhine," for her ability to see into the future like an ancient sibyl. People assumed that a direct link to God gave her knowledge of the future. Convents competed for her to join them, considering her prophetic powers something of a tourist attraction. She received many letters requesting that she look into the future and report what she saw.

Once a woman wrote to ask for help with her sick husband. Hildegard replied, "I see much darkness in him," and urged the woman to prepare to live on without him. Indeed, the man died shortly afterward. Unfortunately, the content of most of her correspondence is lost to us now, but we know that the value of a letter from her, a talisman, could hardly be overestimated.

Hildegard never presented herself as a psychic, but she didn't argue with people who saw her that way. Their belief in her ability to see ahead was most useful for her ulterior motive, which was to get people to lead more virtuous lives. She seems to have played a combination sibyl-Dear Abby-Wizard of Oz role that could easily have gotten her in trouble with religious authorities. She was often misunderstood and ridiculed, and many did condemn her as satanic. Critics scorned her as "Crumplegard," referring to her wrinkled face, or as that "certain old woman further up the Rhine." (As recently as 1984, a Catholic magazine referred to her as a "fruitcake.") But she had friends in high places and was never threatened with being burned as a witch.

The Power of Headaches

Recently doctors have looked again at Hildegard's descriptions of her visions. Her physical symptoms correspond to what we now know to be signs of migraine attacks. These headaches of overwhelming intensity are usually followed by temporary paralysis and blindness—all reported by Hildegard: "I did not die, yet I did not altogether live." When they pass, there is a euphoria, also described by her: "Every sadness and pain vanishes from my memory, so that I am again as a simple maid and not as an old woman." Yet somehow Hildegard managed to recycle her private pain into an ambition that led to groundbreaking achievements.

Hildegard died in 1179 at the age of 81. Most of her remains are in Rudesheim near the Rhine River. Her heart and tongue are at Bingen, where her monastery, the Abbey of St. Hildegard, still thrives.

Nine hundred years after her birth, her extraordinary music is being rediscovered. Several CDs of Hildegard's angelic harmonies have become bestsellers, and people are now marveling at what else she did that was ahead of its time.

Leonardo da Vinci

"I wish to work miracles."

ITALIAN RENAISSANCE ARTIST (1452–1519)
WHOSE SCIENTIFIC DRAWINGS
REVEALED A RICH AND STRIKINGLY
PERCEPTIVE VIEW OF THE FUTURE

In addition to holding an enduring reputation as a great painter and sculptor, Leonardo da Vinci has, in recent years, gained fame as an eerily prophetic thinker.

But Leonardo wasn't a psychic performing feats of magical intuition. There was no divine inspiration involved. Rather, he drew his breathtaking conclusions from science and hard facts. And he had an ability to observe reality that few have equaled.

THE OUTSIDER

The period known as the Renaissance, spanning the fourteen to seventeenth centuries, lifted Europe out of the dark days of the Middle Ages. Horizons broadened. Explorers roamed, redrawing maps that unveiled an earth much vaster than once believed. Scientific discoveries and developments in all the arts revealed human potential to be virtually unlimited. It was a heady time, a "rebirth" (the meaning of *Renaissance*) of classical learning. Italy was the new center of brilliant creativity, drawing inspiration from ancient Greece and Rome. The rest of Europe learned from Italy, and all of Western civilization blossomed.

The ultimate Renaissance man—a person who was brilliantly creative at *everything*—was Leonardo da Vinci.

Born in Italy in 1452, Leonardo stood apart from others in almost every way. He was illegitimate, and so was denied the privileges of children born within a marriage. He received the basic elementary education for boys of his day (reading, writing, and arithmetic) but did not attend one of the new universities. His "university" was the workshop of a local artist, who took him on as a fifteen-year-old apprentice and fostered the young man's talents. Leonardo's flowering artistic genius also isolated him—a genius that would one day lead to such unparalleled creations as the *Mona Lisa* and *The Last Supper.*

In addition, Leonardo was left-handed, a trait thought to be the work of the devil; fastidious (in a smelly age); homosexual, a legal offense that was punishable by death; and a vegetarian (in a world of heavy meat-eaters), who believed that someday murdering animals would be a crime. Most of all, he was a thinker—at a time when a new kind of thinking known as scientific investigation was banned.

As they did during the Middle Ages, religious officials believed that science threatened their authority. Rumors constantly circulated that Leonardo placed science above the Christian faith and even saw himself as a god—the ultimate heresy. But such talk was unjustified: Leonardo was in fact religious and inclined to be almost jealous of God, whom he saw as a better inventor than himself. "I wish to work miracles," he often wrote. He did not, however, conform to *organized* religion, and was such a question mark—all that time alone, sketching

on tiny paper pads he kept in his belt, dissecting dead bodies, boiling herbs—
that the rumors never stopped.

Not Just Any Doodles

Curiosity bubbled freely throughout the Renaissance world, but Leonardo's curiosity was a fountain. Systematically he investigated nearly every topic with an almost unimaginable patience. Then he made drawings, starting from nature and imagining the rest. In his futuristic "notebooks," he amassed over 5,000 pages of drawings.

Much of what Leonardo drew did not technically get invented for centuries: contact lenses, cars, bicycles, expressways, airplanes, helicopters, prefabricated houses, burglarproof locks, automatic door closers, submarines, life preservers, steam engines, and tanks. As technical drawings, there were none more precise and elegant until computer-aided draftsmanship came along five hundred years later. He intended to organize them into a kind of encyclopedia of everything. But (as with so many of his plans) he never got around to it, so the drawings remain loosely arranged by topics.

Nervous about his privacy, he wrote in symbols or backward. His tiny brown writing went from right to left, so that others had to use a mirror to read it. He was paranoid about being caught challenging the Biblical account of creation and many other Church teachings. It is probably no coincidence that his earliest inventing efforts have to do with escape from imprisonment.

"So many things have remained unknown or misinterpreted for centuries!" Leonardo often wrote. Throughout the mind-boggling notebooks, he asked questions no one had ever dreamed of before: Why do we laugh when we're tickled? How can hot and cold running water be installed in a house? Why can't humans fly?

As any good scientist does, Leonardo tested his hypotheses whenever possible by way of firsthand experience. To do a complex medical drawing, for example, he would spend a week or more with a corpse, under conditions few would have tolerated. Alone, he performed at least thirty autopsies (strictly forbidden by the Church), resulting in illustrations so accurate they could still be used in medical textbooks today. He made breakthroughs in cardiology, neurology, osteology, and, especially, ophthalmology—the branch of medicine dealing with the eye.

Sight was to Leonardo the highest sense, the avenue to wisdom—more important than book knowledge. Other scientists of his day declared that the eye projected particles, creating what we see. Leonardo knew that the eye transmitted nothing but instead received rays of light. Others insisted that light filled the world in a single instant. He believed that light traveled. He was able to explain why we perceive the sky as blue and he was the first to point out why stars are visible by night but not by day. He developed a method for observing the eclipse of the sun without hurting your eyes.

Centuries before men landed on the moon, he predicted what they would see: namely, Earth.

WALKING ON WATER

Leonardo's drawings include many engineering feats of irrigation, drainage, and canal-building. He designed sewers and palaces, air-cooling devices, and a self-propelled ship with paddle wheels (three hundred years before the invention of the steam-powered paddleboat). He invented the snorkel, the life preserver, and water shoes, or "Floats for Walking on Water." These were inflated animal skins with wooden floats that were long and light enough to bear a person's weight, as long as you held two sticks to help you keep your balance and move forward.

One sketch is unmistakably a bicycle with pedals, chain, and wheels. Other drawings show cars, propelled by springs powered by a trip-hammer.

Although Leonardo seemed peace loving (he thought war was a *bestialissima pazzia*, a "beastly madness"), he was, nevertheless, a prophet in military science.

As some war was always raging, anyone with engineering or architectural knowledge was expected to aid Italy's defense. Leonardo contributed more than most people: designs for a machine gun, parachutes (made with linen, spruce, and rope), and a flying machine similar to a helicopter; explosives, battering rams, and a way to tunnel noiselessly. He also drew sketches of heavily fortified vehicles—like flying saucers with four wheels—behind which armies could advance. These vehicles did not come into existence until World War I, more than four hundred years later. They were called tanks.

Two of his innovations pleased him above all others. One was his design for a submarine, an invention he was especially secretive about. Always pessimistic about human nature, he worried that enemies would steal his design and figure out how to pierce holes in the submarine. Then the people his invention was intended to protect would drown.

His other primary delight was connected to the notion of flying. Since his teens, Leonardo had been preoccupied with it. Four hundred years before the Wright brothers, he was positive that heavier-than-air objects could be made to fly. At first he thought arm movement was the key. But after carefully observing the muscles used by birds, he realized that legs provided the real power. He tinkered with materials (pinewood strengthened with lime, canvas covered with feathers, leather smeared with grease), shapes (a canoe, a large butterfly, a rowing machine, a windmill, a modern hang glider), mechanisms (pedals, sails, rudders, harnesses), and safety devices (a long wineskin filled with air worn around the waist as a buoy in case one fell in a lake).

Most scientists today agree that his flying machines never actually worked—perhaps he meant them as toys—but there is no question that they sparked other imaginations. They inspired Leonardo, too: in his paintings the angels make aerodynamically correct landings, demonstrating what he'd discovered about principles of flight.

Other accomplishments include laying the basis for modern map-making, and inventing a way to make gold sequins for women's clothes. He intended his various inventions to be systematically manufactured, anticipating the methods of the Industrial Revolution that began more than two hundred years later.

Finally, to get himself out of bed each morning—always a problem for him—he devised a unique kind of alarm clock that worked using water. (Electric alarm clocks would not be invented for four hundred years.)

HOW DID HE KNOW?

Leonardo was so extremely secretive that he did not publish any of his notebooks. If he had, the world might have caught up with him a lot sooner. Instead, after his death in 1519 his drawings were scattered, lost, or accidentally destroyed. Not until about 1800 did they start coming to light and inspiring other visionaries. Thirty-one priceless notebooks have survived and are now kept in various museums.

The most famous of these notebooks is known as the Codex Leicester. It is owned by none other than Bill Gates, who as the founder of Microsoft Corporation, the world's largest producer of computer software, is viewed by many as a modern psychic. At age ten, Gates first encountered Leonardo. "Da Vinci is someone I have admired since I first read about him. . . . He talks about major things to come . . . in a clear, terse fashion." Gates grew up to become America's richest man and purchased the notebook, in 1994, for $30.8 million. The Codex Leicester relates to all things watery—the shape of a dew drop, the intricacies of bubbles, how water flows down steps. It includes diagrams of what look like a working toilet and a steam engine, 250 years before its actual invention.

No one has ever explained how Leonardo could have foreseen so much. He *was* a lifelong student, but many people continue learning throughout their lives. Few, however, explore every field of human knowledge or study things quite so closely as he did.

To Leonardo, seeing was the key. *Saper vedere,* "knowing how to see," was his goal; and he seems to have reached it. Like other people, he would throw stones into the water—but he would be the only one to notice the exact pattern of the rings. (Indeed, in his notebooks he defined the principle of waves.) Such were his patience and his fierce drive to understand that he simply saw things others missed.

In his private life Leonardo may have needed an alarm clock. But in terms of world history, he has been called "a man who wakes too early, while it is still dark and all around are sleeping."

Nostradamus

"The young lion shall overcome the old . . ."

FRENCH PHYSICIAN (1503-1566)
WHO BECAME THE MOST FAMOUS
NAME FOR PREDICTIONS—APPROXIMATELY
HALF OF WHICH HAVE COME TRUE,
ACCORDING TO SCHOLARS

If you lived in France during the 1500s, you would have much to be grateful for. Farmers have finally improved their methods, and with more food around, you will live longer and more prosperously in Europe's biggest country. The religious influence on every area of daily life is starting to break down, and society is taking its first steps toward separating church and government. You actually have some say over which religion you choose to practice. But you must be careful to avoid murder or torture by other religious groups: Catholics and Protestants are fighting bloody battles for supremacy, and both persecute Jews.

One thing has persisted throughout the European Renaissance: a love for the occult. Now it is stronger than ever. Perhaps astrology and other occult beliefs provide comfort because they unite people rather than divide them, as religion is doing. Perhaps they are easier to understand than many of the new ideas being circulated, and people hate to let them go. Even in this age of enlightenment, some thirty-thousand fortune-tellers of various types work just in Paris, the sparkling French capital. The queen, Catherine de Medicis, has at least four astrologers at court at all times. Then there is that certain French doctor capturing the attention of *everyone*.

He is Michel de Nostredame—better known as Nostradamus—and he is making the art of prediction world famous.

A REBEL

Born in 1503, Nostradamus grew up as an outsider. His parents practiced their Jewish faith in secret, after publicly converting to Catholicism under threat of banishment. Priests at school were always angry at him for upholding the Copernican theory that the world is round. They also faulted his obsession with astrology. His nickname in medical school was "Little Astrologer." Astrology was perfectly acceptable in that era. Known as the "celestial science," it was even part of basic medical training. But no one studied it in more detail than Nostradamus.

As a doctor, he specialized in the bubonic plague, the highly infectious disease that swept across Europe and Asia, killing millions. Known as the Black Death, it inflicted large black blisters and other painful symptoms upon its victims. Other doctors used bleeding to treat the plague (and everything else). But Nostradamus, guided by his vast readings of Islamic material, prescribed fresh air, clean water, and his famous rose pills: green cyprus sawdust, cloves, and aloe, mixed with rose-petal powder (which happened to be full of vitamin C). Valiantly, almost single-handedly, he cured whole towns. Then the plague claimed his wife and two children. Friends and family turned against him for being unable to save his own family. He was ordered by religious authorities to face trial for a humorous remark about demons he'd made years before.

One night, he packed his mule with his belongings and fled. When he returned ten years later, he had started to gain respect for a new talent: predictions. Rumors spread that his energy had gone inward, and a gift for prophecy had emerged. He married a rich widow, had six more children, and dove whole-heartedly into looking at the future.

THE RITUALS OF NOSTRADAMUS

Nostradamus converted the chilly top floor of his house in Salon into a study full of books on the occult. He reached it by way of a spiral stone staircase and ruled it off-limits to others. Spying neighbors noticed the light from his candle at all hours of the night. He needed only four to five hours of sleep, and the rest of the time he spent working.

Using the Oracle at Delphi as a model, he placed a brass bowl of steaming water and fragrant oils on a tripod; some accounts say he sat on the tripod himself. Staring at the water, or at a fire, helped him to focus. Then he busied himself looking up horoscopes from the past, using maps that showed how stars and other heavenly bodies were positioned on particular dates. By means still mysterious, he then calculated when and where, or on what latitude, major elements of those past events would reoccur. (There was always going to be "another Hannibal," "another Nero," and so on.) He asked for divine help in summoning up actual names and dates, after which he fleshed out the results by way of further research, more astrological conjecturing, meditation, and obscure techniques he had picked up during his travels.

He began writing down what he saw, shaping his visions into verse. His masterpiece is *Centuries*, an ambitious collection of a thousand rhymed prophecies foretelling the entire future of the world.

HARD TO READ

Sometimes the verses in *Centuries* are enigmatic, in the manner of the Oracle at Delphi's verses. Sometimes they're quite specific. To confuse the authorities during a time when anything pagan, or pre-Christian, was punishable by death, Nostradamus wrote in many languages and scrambled his words. He also made some verses obscure to avoid hurting feelings or injuring anyone. Some people even think he jumbled pages by throwing them into the air and reordering them according to how they landed.

Literally hundreds of books have been written to explain *Centuries*. Industrious Nostradamus scholars have invested years in deciphering its verses. To read the book today you must be a sort of mental contortionist. It helps to have extensive knowledge of sixteenth-century French (including lots of esoteric wordplay) as well as Arabic, Latin, Hebrew, Italian, and Greek.

Nostradamus's writings may sound garbled. But then *Centuries* began coming true during the doctor's own lifetime. He predicted an unusual demise for the king of France, Henry II:

> *The young lion shall overcome the old*
> *In warlike fields in single duel;*
> *In a cage of gold he will pierce his eyes,*
> *Two wounds one, then die, a cruel death.*

Four years later, Henry was in a jousting tournament with the captain of his Scottish Guards. The younger knight's jousting spear splintered, and one point slipped into the king's throat. The other plunged through his golden helmet, through his eye, and into his brain. In horrible pain, Henry died that night.

The prediction's stunning accuracy made Nostradamus instantly notorious at the age of fifty-six.

The ignorant and superstitious jumped to the conclusion that he must have been a witch under the devil's power. In fact, the first use of the very word *prediction* dates to an attack on Nostradamus from this time. Some speculated that the doctor had plotted to kill the king; and the night of Henry's death, angry crowds burned Nostradamus in effigy, as a message to the authorities. Later, Catholic and Protestant extremists regularly stoned his house, forcing him at times to live elsewhere.

To the majority of people, however, Nostradamus couldn't have been more intriguing. The reading public devoured his books. Some thought he was even the voice of God. Queen Catherine summoned him to Paris, where he became her personal astrologer. He did horoscopes for her children—a ticklish task, as he had previously foretold a tragic end for each. Later she had King Charles IX give Nostradamus the title of Counselor and Physician in Ordinary. Foreign ambassadors reported that the court was overcome by "Nostradamania," ruling out talk of anything else. He became the toast of all Europe's courts, with many friends in high places.

Some of these "friends" enjoyed testing him. Once, the lord of a grand manor asked him which of two pigs in a corral would be served for dinner that night. Nostradamus is supposed to have said, "We will eat the black pig, but a wolf will eat the white."

Secretly, the lord ordered his cook to kill the white pig. The cook left the kitchen at some point, and came back to find the lord's pet wolf cub eating the white pig. Quickly he fetched the black one and prepared dinner—but later that night he was forced to admit the seer had been right.

SORTING IT OUT

Most Nostradamus experts seem to think that around half of his predictions have come true. The trouble is that they disagree about just which predictions apply to which events.

Most agree that he named the specific date of the great London fire (1666) and he seemed to get right certain details of the French Revolution (1789–1799). He referred to Louis Pasteur (born in 1822) and Pasteur's scientific breakthroughs; and he appeared able to foresee future approaches to treating diseases (such as the plague) and gear his techniques to them.

The experts believe that he also predicted the rise of Adolf Hitler (born in 1889). Besides referring to "a captain of Greater Germany" in terms that seemed to fit, he used the name "Hister" three times in *Centuries*. This is not only close to the German dictator's name but is the Latin name for the Austrian river Danube, near where Hitler grew up.

In the 1940s the wife of Joseph Goebbels, Hitler's Minister of Propaganda, was obsessed with the occult. She ran into Nostradamus's references in her reading and showed them to Goebbels. He seized on them, interpreted them to predict that Germany would rule the world, and had special Nostradamus leaflets printed. During World War II, trying to demoralize Germany's enemies, he ordered thousands of these leaflets dropped over Belgium and France. In the same areas, Britain had *its* planes drop Nostradamus verses, slanted to predict victory for Britain and the other Allies. In the United States, meanwhile, newsreels proclaimed Nostradamus a prophetic champion of democracy.

The names and dates in other prophecies are much murkier. Nostradamus mentions three Antichrists that would move humanity toward total destruction. The French emperor Napoleon and Hitler are generally agreed to be the first two, but whether Iraqi leader Saddam Hussein is the third is a big topic of debate among Nostradamaniacs. The doctor refers several times to the "three brothers" annihilated by the Antichrists; many have wanted to view these as the Kennedys (the assassinated John F. and Robert F., plus their brother Joe, the first choice of their father to become president, until he was killed during World War II). Nostradamaniacs also debate his prediction about a city that sounds like New York being attacked with fire from the sky—which some interpret as meaning destroyed in a nuclear war.

Recent events said to be foretold include the 1969 moon landing; AIDS ("a very great plague will come with a great scab. Relief near but the remedies far away"); the Gulf War (with very eerie parallels to his prophecies); civil war in Yugoslavia; the *Challenger* shuttle disaster ("the nine set apart . . . their fate determined on departure"); the Hale-Bopp Comet; and the death of England's Princess Diana.

In May 1988, Nostradamus scholars warned people on the West Coast to prepare for the massive earthquake scientists had been forecasting for some time. Their panic resulted from *The Man Who Saw Tomorrow*, an American documentary about Nostradamus. According to an interpretation presented in the film, the doctor specified a great quake for that date. Though some people did evacuate the coast, the "Big One" failed to materialize.

In the land of Nostradamus studies, people believe that his verses with no apparent meaning are events that have not yet occurred. Actually, his "prophecies" tend to be best understood only after the event has happened, seldom before. Are these truly predictions? Some people think he can be interpreted to mean almost anything. But others study him anyway—if he was right about so much during the past four hundred years, he may provide further assistance. Rulers ever since Nostradamus's own time have combed the verses for hints of the future.

Centuries has been continuously available in print for hundreds of years, a distinction it shares with few other books, most notably, the Bible.

Recent events show that Nostradamus was a favorite with the Japanese doomsday cult, the True Teaching of Aum, which in 1995 planned a nerve-gas attack on the Tokyo subway system. They interpreted his predictions about the end of the world would occur in a way that fit their own scenario exactly.

THE END

It's not clear whether Nostradamus really did predict the end of the world. He envisioned many natural disasters and great wars around the year 2000. He saw everyone in the world being numbered, recorded and categorized—which fits in with some people's fear about the growing amount of private information the government has about them. He did seem to indicate some kind of apocalypse around 2828. But he also stated specifically in a letter that his prophecies cover the history of the world to the year 3797. In addition, he left behind enigmatic statements about visions he had of events up to the year 8000.

Nostradamus's last prediction, in 1566, was about his own end: "On his return from the Embassy, the King's gift put in place. He will do nothing more. He will be gone to God. Close relatives, friends, brothers by blood will find him completely dead near the bed and the bench."

Months after that prediction, Nostradamus returned from a trip to court in Paris. King Charles had just given him a promotion, with privileges and a high salary. The next morning his family found his body, lying across the bench he had built to help himself get in and out of bed. Nostradamus was dead at age sixty-three.

From the
Twenty Thousand Leagues Under the Sea
Around the Worl
Phileas
Master of the World
mysterious &
which doubtless
forgotten. Not to
rumours which agitated the
to this
log books

Jules Verne

"A new kind of sensation."

INFLUENTIAL FRENCH WRITER (1828-1905)
WHO MADE A CAREER OUT OF
FANTASIZING ABOUT THE FUTURE

Gas lamps and candles produce a feeble light. Still, using their glow to write his books by, French author Jules Verne was able to see . . . cars cruising along freeways, manned capsules floating into outer space, and submarines surging through the deep seas. Quiet in his armchair, he envisioned helicopters, the atomic bomb, TV, computers (which he called "totalizers"), color photography, fax machines ("photographic telegraphs"), radios, bright electric lights. . . .

There was one fascinating conundrum about Verne's books: In the time when he was writing—the mid 1800s—none of these things had been invented. People got around by horses, not cars. Even in a fancy city like Paris, roads were crude, and rutted with horse tracks. And there were still decades of darkness to endure before the use of electricity would become common.

So how on earth did Verne do it?

A Dizzying Age of Discovery

The invention of the steam engine, in 1769, ushered in a phenomenon known as the Industrial Revolution. With engines to harness the surging power of steam, large-scale production was possible. Over the next hundred years, people left their farms and flocked to the cities for factory jobs. The market for manufactured goods flourished. Canals and roads were built to transport these goods. Impossible notions seemed suddenly possible, like entirely new methods of transportation: railroads and steamships. By the 1800s, the air buzzed with talk about fresh ideas, more inventions, and the breakthroughs occurring almost daily in science.

Born in 1828, Jules Verne was more interested, as a child, in geography and literature than in all the scientific innovation that surrounded him. However, he *was* fascinated with machines and would stand for hours at construction sites, watching machines operate. He went on to study law (reluctantly), work as a stockbroker, and write musical comedies.

Then, in his mid-thirties, Verne turned to writing novels for young people. The book that put him on the map was his first: *Five Weeks in a Balloon.* It was about three men who explore the uncharted lands of danger-filled Africa in a unique way—by balloon. Verne had never seen Africa, a place from which explorers didn't always return. He had also never been in a balloon. Though eighty years had passed since the first manned balloon flight, balloons were too difficult to control to be efficient for travel. Verne knew virtually nothing about them.

It just sounded exciting to him—"a new kind of sensation."

Sensational Stories

A few years later, Verne's novel *Twenty Thousand Leagues Under the Sea* used other sensations to pull readers irresistibly into the sea. He wrote:

> *The year 1866 was signalized by a remarkable incident, a mysterious and puzzling*

phenomenon, which doubtless no one has yet forgotten. . . . For some time past vessels had been met by "an enormous thing," a long object, spindle-shaped, occasionally phosphorescent, and infinitely larger and more rapid in its movements than a whale.

The "thing" turns out to be a deep-sea submarine—although *real* submarines wouldn't be navigating freely in the open seas for another thirty years. Yet Verne's heroes travel all around the world in one, after they are captured by the mysterious Captain Nemo. Clearly Verne was growing fascinated by science, especially the way that new transportation had the power to transform the world.

Books such as this, *A Voyage to the Center of the Earth,* and *Around the World in 80 Days* gained Verne worldwide fame. Some hundred more adventures were forthcoming.

No one has ever explained the gulf between Verne's life and his fantasies. He was known as quiet, passive, not particularly pleasant to be around, hypochondriacal, and hardworking. Other than sailing in his beloved sailboat, he seldom traveled. He thought fishing was barbaric and went hunting just once. Over a third of his novels have to do with the United States, but he spent only five days here. He lived in an isolated country house, where his study was as simple as a monk's cell. In it was a bed, so he could be at work before dawn. Disliking the newfangled typewriter, he wrote everything by hand. He also avoided telephones and denounced bicycles.

Nevertheless, Verne's use of science in his novels was wild, extravagant, and splendidly high-tech. His plots zoomed his legions of fans literally everywhere: to jungles, deserts, mountains, and their unexplored corners; to flying islands, outer space, the North and South Poles, the center of the earth, ice fields, volcanoes, asteroids, mine shafts, and underwater caves. During a time when real-life explorers were penetrating some of these very areas—the deepest jungles and most remote deserts around the world—Verne explored by way of the printed page, safe in his solitariness.

Verne did not consider himself an expert on science or the future. He simply wanted to write escapist stories—at a steady two volumes a year—that young people could learn something from. But once science began attracting him, he read nonstop. Whenever he was in doubt about a fact, he left his armchair and went to town to consult the experts. Through the power of imagination, he translated his ultimately considerable knowledge of science into fiction that still thrills readers over a century later.

SPOOKY PARALLELS

On the official U.S. map of the far side of the moon, there is a site called the Jules Verne Crater. Why?

Because Verne wrote a novel in 1865 called *From the Earth to the Moon*. In it, he describes a manned space capsule in a way that foretold Apollo 8, which was launched as the first manned lunar flight in 1968. And of all the places on earth to choose from Verne had chosen the swampy terrain of Tampa, a city in Florida, from which to propel his heroes into space with a huge "gun." Apollo 8 astronauts found it eerie also to be launched into space from Florida. They traveled at almost the same speed as Verne's heroes and endured a similarly small capsule equipped with similarly described condensed food. Verne even anticipated a safe splashdown in the Pacific—just like Apollo 8's.

The three Americans aboard Apollo 8 reported that they never stopped thinking of Verne. One wrote to Verne's great-grandson: "Your illustrious grandfather . . . not only imagined what exploits were possible for man but even how they might be accomplished, down to the finest details. Who can say how many of the world's space scientists were inspired, consciously or unconsciously, by their boyhood reading of the works of Jules Verne?"

Many twentieth-century pioneers do credit the writer with invigorating their own imaginations. "Jules Verne guides me," said explorer Admiral Richard Byrd about his polar journeys. President Theodore Roosevelt read all of his books, and so did engineer and rocket scientist Wernher von Braun.

Many writers cite Verne as the "Father of Science Fiction." Science fiction—

stories about how technology affects humans—was a new literary genre most appropriate to Verne and his time. He was able to take ideas not yet quite real—the elevator, for example, previewed in New York in 1857—and envision whole worlds of skyscrapers and huge mansions powered by nothing but elevators. Verne treated thoughtfully the consequences of technology—its use and abuse, and the power of government to break spirits with it. Wrote science-fiction star Ray Bradbury: "We are all, in one way or another, the children of Jules Verne."

Verne's stories have been adapted again and again for movies and TV. One of the first movies ever made in France, in 1902, was based on *From the Earth to the Moon*. In 1997 there were not one but two network TV remakes of *Twenty Thousand Leagues Under the Sea*. The classic 1954 Disney version influenced the look of Star Trek and James Bond movies. Several Disney theme-park rides are Verne-inspired as well.

His influence shows little sign of dying out. The creators of the CD-ROM game *Myst*, which has sold millions since 1993, have repeatedly held up *The Mysterious Island* by Verne as their inspiration for the game. *The New York Times* recently referred to him as the "patron saint of cyberspace," the kind of uncharted and unpredictable landscape that he probably would have adored. Indeed, in one book he wrote that people were no longer reading newspapers, but were instead getting their own personal news from something that sounds very much like the Internet.

"NO ONE WOULD BELIEVE IT"

In 1989, the author's great-grandson found an old manuscript in a rusty bronze safe on the Verne family estate. It was a novel that Verne had written in 1863 called *Paris in the Twentieth Century*. His editor had rejected the manuscript as too grim to print: "My dear Verne . . . no one today would believe this prophecy." In fact, the book is a remarkable catalog of technology not known at the time he was writing.

In Verne's twentieth-century landscape, cars ("gas cabs") have replaced horses. They coast along smooth streets made of asphalt. Up on elevated platforms run silent, pollution-free trains, propelled by compressed air. Skyscrapers, equipped with elevators, are seventy to eighty stories high. Electricity makes the department stores glow brilliantly. It also serves as an instrument for capital punishment (our electric chair) for those caught by way of sophisticated burglar-catching devices. Millions listen at the same time to music transported through the air (our radio), and they use inventions that sound like copiers, calculators, and fax machines.

Verne died in 1905, not far enough into this century to see how much he had predicted would come to pass. Not until 1996 was *Paris in the Twentieth Century* published in English. Readers found the technology amazing, but other aspects of the novel depressing. Hordes of homeless wander the streets. Overpopulation is a plague, and machines are replacing humans at work. Charismatic leaders control the world with wars and flying killing machines. Everyone is bombarded by commercial advertising. Quantities of chemical products belch into the air. The hero ends up weeping himself into unconsciousness in a cemetery.

MAKING THE FUTURE

Not everything Verne foresaw has come true (yet).

Some of his more fanciful notions include doctors who get paid only when their patients are well; global climate control; food piped into homes; and mechanized dressing rooms that wash, shave, and dress their pampered occupants in clothes of spun metal. He imagined a heavy tax on bachelors that would increase marriages, and so many babies that 500-nurse-power baby-feeding machines would be necessary. Music would sound like an orchestra tuning up, with no melody or rhythm. Advertisements would be projected onto clouds. There would be air cars, air buses, and air trains, as well as personal-energy accumulators that provide unlimited power. People would travel from

Paris to New York in 295 minutes by trans-Atlantic underground tubes. Verne foresaw interplanetary communication and the discovery of "Olympus," a planet beyond Neptune's orbit.

Such possible wrong turns wouldn't have mattered to Verne, who saw himself as a popular writer, not a prophet. And they don't matter to those who appreciate Verne's knack for getting so many things right. The question for those trying to explain such extraordinary foresight is: Did Verne really see the future, or were his fictional descriptions so detailed that people used them as blueprints?

In other words, could it be that Verne was *making* the future? Did he so entice his young readers that they started to do the very things he had dreamed up?

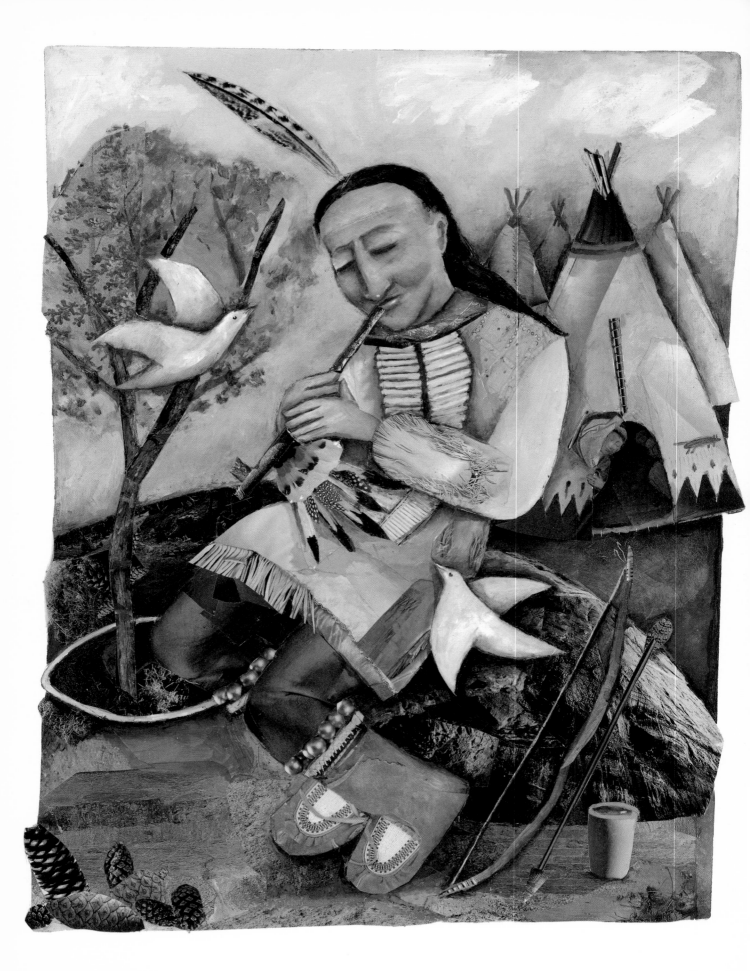

Nicholas Black Elk

"Sometimes dreams are wiser than waking."

An American Indian
medicine man (1863-1950)
who experienced a vision
when he was nine that became
a cry for peace

As a child Nicholas Black Elk rode horseback freely over the plains with the other members of his tribe. He was a proud member of the Oglala band of the Lakota Sioux Nation.

As an adult he lived confined on a reservation. His tribe was near extinction. European settlers had shattered the American Indians' way of life. And Black Elk had experienced the most nightmarish phase of this destruction—a phase he had foreseen years earlier.

The 12-Day Coma

To be an American Indian in the late 1800s was to be powerless against harsh change. You were in the torturous process of losing your ancestral lands and your way of life. The white settlers had taken away your language, your religion, and all your ways of expressing identity. If you were "lucky," they used laws against you. They made the traditional Lakota way of life illegal and gave thirty-year prison terms to leaders caught conducting ceremonies in their native language. If you were unlucky, they used violence. You lost family members and friends, or your own life. Millions of Indians all across the United States were slaughtered. The government justified its inhumane treatment with phrases like "manifest destiny." White settlers felt that God intended them to dominate the new land by any means necessary.

Born in 1863, Black Elk was aware at an early age of the forcible change enveloping his people. His family experienced times of pain and fear mixed with moments of defiance and hope. A more thoughtful boy than most, Black Elk always felt himself haunted by the unusual. He said he could understand birds when they talked, for example, and often had a feeling he was being called by unseen forces.

Then, when he was nine years old, he fell without explanation into a sudden coma. During the twelve days he was unconscious, this is what he saw:

A white cloud whisked him from Earth and into the heavens. He was met by forty-eight horses of black, white, red, and yellow—twelve each for west, north, east, and south. They led Black Elk to a tepee with a rainbow over its door. Inside were six ancient grandfathers, or holy men.

The first grandfather, representing the west, gave Black Elk a cup of water and a bow. The water symbolized the power to sustain life, and the bow indicated the power to destroy life. The second grandfather, the north, gave him a white wing and sage, the sacred herb. The wing symbolized the cleansing, enduring power of snow, and the sage was for honesty and healing sustenance. The third grandfather, the red dawn of the east, said he would have the power to awaken others. He gave Black Elk the sacred pipe, or the power of peace that comes through knowledge. The fourth grandfather, the south, gave him a bright red stick sprouting leaves, representing the sacredness of life. He told of a tree that would grow in the center of the nation.

Now a yellow hoop appeared in the dream, representing the cycle of life. The fifth grandfather, the sky, became an eagle and told Black Elk that all sky things—birds, winds, stars—would help him. The sixth, Mother Earth, told him that the power of the earth would be with him.

All the grandfathers commanded Black Elk to set his stick in the center of the hoop, where the tree would bloom. But before he could do so, Black Elk saw the earth getting sick, the air and water becoming dirty, humans and animals growing frightened. An evil blue man—representing greed, dishonesty, selfishness—was empowering, or causing, the sickness.

It seemed to Black Elk that the vision contained the whole history of his people. He saw the time when they all followed the "good red road"—that is, they looked after one another and performed traditional songs, ceremonies, and dances. Then he saw fighting and war take over, followed by poverty and despair. He saw the present, with people traveling the "black road." Everybody was for himself, making up his own rules.

He saw the free spirit of the mystic Indian warriors of the plains become nothing more than a captive eagle in the white man's zoo.

In the dream, though, Black Elk was able to kill the blue man and plant the bright red stick. He became a Sun Dance tree, a cottonwood, under which children of all nations gathered. The sacred hoop of his people was only one of many hoops joined to make one great hoop. All things grew fresh and healthy again, and the entire life cycle of Earth was complete.

UNRAVELING THE VISION

"Sometimes dreams are wiser than waking," Black Elk commented much later. But as a nine-year-old he found the vision overwhelming. For most of his life he didn't even speak of it, for fear of being thought foolish. It took him years to understand its meaning. Certainly it alerted him to the importance of protecting the Indian way of life. But how could he explain this persuasively to others? What could one boy do?

Black Elk continued to witness the downward spiral of his people without feeling he could help. At age thirteen, he fought in the Battle of Little Big Horn. He shared its triumph with Crazy Horse, the revered chief of the Oglala Sioux, to whom he was related. But the victory quickly soured—it led directly to the confinement of Indians on reservations.

From then on, artificial boundaries imposed by whites kept Indians imprisoned. Instead of roaming the plains, they now lived in unhealthy conditions in square, cheaply built gray houses. Without access to their traditional methods of getting food and supporting themselves, most fell into miserable poverty. Black Elk experienced the despair firsthand at the Pine Ridge reservation in South Dakota, the new home to the Oglala.

The genocide peaked in 1890, with the massacre at Wounded Knee, a creek in South Dakota. During this last major battle of the war against the Indians, the cavalry killed several hundred Sioux warriors, women, and children. The massacre dealt a deathblow to the Indian spirit. Ten years later, out of an estimated 12.5 million Indians in North America before the arrival of whites, there were only 250,000 left.

Heartbroken, twenty-seven-year-old Black Elk sought to realize the bright future in his vision. The only hope to coexist with whites seemed to be to learn more about them. Perhaps, he thought, the relationship could be improved by integrating some of their beliefs into the Indian way of life.

With this as his explanation, he joined Buffalo Bill's Wild West Show as a dancer. He traveled all around Europe, performing for England's Queen Victoria, among many others. Black Elk encountered one surprise after another: Christianity, big houses, and lights so bright that stars could not be seen at night. Unlike Indians, these people did not seem to look out for one another. Some had more of everything than they could use, while crowds of others were starving. Few cared about the sick and helpless, or the well-being of future generations. Relationships to the land and its creatures seemed upside down—whites slaughtered buffalo, for example, for reasons having nothing to with obtaining food.

Far from finding a better way to live, Black Elk came to the conclusion that non-Indian ways were unhealthy to the point of insanity.

LIVING IN TWO WORLDS

Black Elk returned to his tribe to practice traditional Lakota rituals. He started to gain respect for his leadership and, especially, for his healing ability. As a noted medicine man, he seemed to have special power to cure the sick: "The visions and the ceremonies had only made me like a hole through which the power could come." He mixed with tourists, reenacting scenes of Lakota life in pageants, performing for crowds that gathered to watch workers carve the great monument at Mount Rushmore.

Living in a one-room log house on the Pine Ridge reservation, he had six children, from marriages first to Katie War Bonnet and then to Anna Brings White. His only daughter, Lucy Looks Twice, reported that his health declined even while he healed others; he became partly crippled and almost completely blind (from an accident with gunpowder), and suffered from stomach trouble.

To some people's astonishment, Black Elk eventually converted to a white man's religion, Catholicism, and became a very active missionary. The only explanation he ever gave was, "My children had to live in this world." The conversion seemed to be his way of adapting to the here and now.

All this time, though, Black Elk continued to dwell on his vision. He called himself "a pitiful old man who has done nothing." In one final attempt to make his vision real and to bring it to his community, Black Elk decided to tell his life story at age sixty-nine. The dream would be its centerpiece. It's not clear how much Black Elk had talked to other Indians about his vision before deciding to present it to the world. But he agreed to work with John Neihardt, a white writer who often wrote about Indian life and whose sincerity impressed him. Black Elk's son Ben, who knew English fairly well, acted as interpreter. Standing Bear, his oldest and best friend, was on hand to verify that Black Elk was telling the truth.

Neihardt claimed he was working on "the first absolutely Indian book thus far written."

FILLING WITH SINGING BIRDS

Unfortunately, no one noticed the book called *Black Elk Speaks* when it was published in 1932. It quickly went out of print.

Years later, shortly before Black Elk died in 1950, he and Neihardt climbed into the Black Hills of South Dakota. Atop the rocky precipice of Harney Peak, Black Elk performed a pipe ceremony beseeching the six powers of the great vision. He lamented that his vision was going to be lost forever, but even now he still had hope: "It may be true that some little root of the sacred tree still lives. Nourish it then, that it may leaf and bloom and fill with singing birds."

Black Elk's vision did not die. Eleven years after his death, *Black Elk Speaks* was reissued. This time it reached a wider audience, a new generation of Indians who appreciated it as a basic book about their identity. Then, after Neihardt told the story of Black Elk on the Dick Cavett TV show in 1971, sales took off. The book became famous not just as an Indian classic, but as a Bible for young people. Many were on a spiritual quest during the 1970s, a time of huge social upheaval. They heard the Oglala leader's words less as a prediction than as a cry for peace. A whole chorus of American Indian voices have reported their visions of the future; but the power of Black Elk's words made his voice rise above all others.

Now his vision is studied in colleges across the United States. He is a major influence on contemporary Indian activists (who have mastered a new "weapon"—the Internet—to spread Black Elk's words), psychologists, anthropologists, and historians. As the environmental movement has surged in recent years, more people are dedicating themselves to healing the earth and to a spirituality based on nature. In 1978 Congress passed the Freedom of Religion Act, legalizing the traditional Lakota way of life at last. Recently it designated Harney Peak in the Black Hills as "Black Elk Wilderness."

And the American Indian population is no longer shrinking. According to the U.S. Census Bureau, it is expanding and will reach 2.5 million by the year 2003.

Perhaps the sacred tree is beginning to bloom at last.

H. G. Wells

"I told you so."

ENGLISH NOVELIST (1866–1946)
FAMED AS "THE MAN WHO
INVENTED TOMORROW" IN HIS
INNOVATIVE SCIENCE FICTION

"No one would have believed, in the last years of the nineteenth century, that human affairs were being watched keenly and closely by intelligences greater than man's . . ."

Those ominous "intelligences" are Martians—repulsive giant brains whose intentions are pure evil. Their planet is exhausted, and they want ours. Converging on England, they pulverize anything and anyone in their way. Town by town, England disintegrates, powerless against weapons no one on Earth has ever seen. The Martians blast humanity with poison gas, efficient and deadly robots, massive guns that shoot pillars of heat. Too hysterical to fight back, people simply flee. Panic cancels out civilized behavior—people will do anything to their neighbors in order to survive. And the depth of human selfishness is perhaps the scariest thing of all . . .

FROM TEXTBOOKS TO TIME MACHINES

Actually, this quote and description are the famous first sentence and the plot of a novel called *The War of the Worlds*, and it was dreamed up by Englishman Herbert George Wells.

Real life in the Great Britain of his day was tumultuous in more mundane ways. The most industrialized country in the world was leading the way in scientific research, exploration, and everyday conveniences. It was also leading the way in hardship. The Industrial Revolution that had begun a century earlier had turned out to have a dark side: disastrous pollution of the air and water, a cruel system of child labor in factories, the creation of miserable slums resulting from too many people cramming into cities, the loss of personal bonds with relatives and neighbors. Help for these serious problems was not forthcoming from the government. England's Queen Victoria presided from 1837 all the way to 1901 over a society ever more strict and bland in its thinking.

H. G. Wells could envision the future beyond Victoria, and he for one dreamed of revolt.

Born in 1866, "Bertie" Wells was sickly and poor, without many advantages in life. He left school at age fourteen, but continued to read voraciously, especially about science. After several menial jobs, he won a scholarship to study biology and became a teacher.

The first book he published was *A Textbook of Biology*, after which he described himself as "writing away for dear life." Obsessed with the future, he shifted from nonfiction about science to stories about how imaginary inventions would affect humans. Unfortunately, British publishers believed that stuffy England was not ready for his brand of science fiction. He amassed a huge collection of rejection slips.

Then came the acceptance and publication of a novel called *The Time Machine*.

Wells wrote about a traveler who explores 800,000 years into the future with the aid of the new machine he has invented. Earth has become a dying planet under a huge red sun. Evil workers live underground, venturing out only to eat the beautiful and wealthy people. Eventually the only surviving things are creepy giant crabs.

Though Wells's vision of time travel was nothing but depressing, the novel was an immediate hit. It appeared that people were ready for this kind of escapist literature after all, which bore just enough resemblance to their real lives. Wells's financial worries were over.

After establishing the time machine as a basic sci-fi concept, Wells went on to new ideas in *The Island of Doctor Moreau*, *The Invisible Man*, *The First Man in the Moon*, *The Shape of Things to Come*, and other books. He wrote over a million words in all, more than William Shakespeare and Charles Dickens put together.

Wells earned credit, along with Jules Verne, as a co-creator of science fiction—a new way of looking at the future combining stories with science and technology. Like Verne, Wells found inspiration in the rush of daily discoveries. The two writers strongly denied influencing each other, though. Wells accused Verne of bad writing, and Verne accused Wells of bad science.

Wells envisioned the future in small ways—"babble machines that told news" (our radio), and machines resembling our VCRs, TVs, and computers—to large (superhighways, overcrowded cities, nuclear war). He even crafted prophecies about prophecies: Experts would soon be making scientific forecasts that were just as detailed as geologists' descriptions of the past. We should be able to predict—scientifically— what will happen in the next twelve hundred years, he thought.

Wells wrote to entertain, even to crusade, but he wasn't trying to accurately predict the future. Usually he was writing fantasy, taking his imagination on soaring flights. Nevertheless, some of his most bizarre notions did become true in some way.

· · ·

ALIEN INVASION

Creatures from Mars invade England in *The War of the Worlds*, one of Wells's best-sellers. Four years before its publication in 1898, Mars was positioned unusually close to Earth. Newspapers reported much observation and speculation about life there. Wells got the idea to invent a whole new type of story, all about interplanetary war.

To make the events more real, Wells wrote in a slyly documentary style. He tied his tale to sites familiar to his readers. The bicycle had just been invented, much to Wells's delight ("When I see an adult on a bicycle, I do not despair for the future of the human race"), and he was learning to ride as he worked on this novel. He biked all over to find places to describe. He took private pleasure in having Martians wreck neighborhoods he didn't like, "killing my neighbors in painful and eccentric ways," selecting one area "for feats of particular atrocity."

The opening sentences of the novel are its most famous. Forty years later, in 1938, they were memorably read aloud by American actor Orson Welles. Broadcasting the novel on the radio, the actor updated the story and replaced the references to England with places in New Jersey. Radio listeners went into shock. Assuming that the actor was reading the day's news, many leaped to the conclusion that Martians had just invaded America—for real. Before Orson Welles could get very far, telephone lines jammed. Thousands of frightened listeners left their homes and poured into the streets. Normally rational, civilized people so lost their cool that the National Guard nearly had to be called out to restore calm. It was a wild scene H. G. Wells himself could have written, a lesson in the energy of his words. It was also a valuable lesson about the power of this newly invented mass medium: Radio could actually shape behavior.

With *The War of the Worlds*, Wells established the image of Martians and numerous sci-fi conventions still popular to this day. The people who created *Star Trek* and countless alien invasion movies, including the 1996 film *Independence Day*, probably owe their earliest nightmares to this novel.

The book also foreshadows the use of poison gas warfare (which came true during World War I), laserlike weapons, and industrial robots. Wells tended to be at his most accurate when foreseeing new ways people would kill one another. In other books, he accurately foresaw developments in the military use of aircraft, aerial bombing, and tanks ("land iron-clads"). In 1911 Wells was the first to envision fully a new kind of weapon—an atomic bomb used to destroy whole cities. A key figure in the real atom bomb's development, Hungarian physicist Leo Szilard, later credited Wells for his inspiration.

"A BUBBLING CREATIVE MIND"

For a small man who dressed badly and often acted unkindly, Wells had an active romantic schedule. One woman said simply that he "made everyone else in the world seem a dull dog." She called him "the most bubbling creative mind that the sun and moon have shone upon since the days of Leonardo da Vinci." His life was crowded with relationships with some notable women of his day (including novelist Rebecca West, birth control pioneer Margaret Sanger, and Soviet spy Baroness Moura Budberg).

Complete freedom intoxicated Wells. Marriage? Only if you wanted to be a parent, he felt. All other relationships were no one else's business. With his attitudes, Wells was way ahead of his straightlaced time. Before most people did so, he talked about social equality, world peace, population control, pollution, and the decimation of forests and of entire species. An enormous influence on his generation and the one after, he made revolt against Victorian codes of behavior seem possible. "Queen Victoria," he once insisted, "was like a great paperweight that for half a century sat upon men's minds, and when she was removed their ideas began to blow about all over the place haphazardly."

BLEAK WORLD AHEAD

Wells was of two minds about our future. At first, he'd hoped that humans could evolve into higher life-forms, adapting to changing circumstances with their knowledge and education. Sometimes he sensed a "progress that will go on, with an ever-widening and ever more confident stride, forever." A benevolent modern government could take care of fear, hunger, and other "primary stresses." This would leave people free for thrilling feats of technology.

But the devastation of World War I shook his faith. By World War II, when some sixty million people died in the worst conflict ever known, he started to lose any feelings of optimism. In these later years, his darker side took over: "The future is still black and blank—a vast ignorance." He concluded that the best we could hope for was to face our destiny "with dignity and mutual aid and charity, without hysteria, meanness and idiotic misrepresentations of each other's motives."

Wells considered the American bombing of Hiroshima and Nagasaki in 1945 the worst tragedy that he had lived to see. Depressed that World War II had given birth to the atomic age, he died the following year at age seventy-nine.

Not everything Wells wrote about came true. He had envisioned houses that by 2000 would have self-cleaning windows and easy-to-sweep floors; architects by then would "have the sense and ability to round off the angle between wall and floor." He doubted the usefulness of the submarine— he couldn't imagine it "doing anything but suffocating its crew and floundering at sea." And most agree that his concept of time travel is far-fetched.

Still, he made many forecasts accurate enough to earn fame as "the man who invented tomorrow." His novels played a robust part in the literary tradition of imagining the road ahead. At his funeral, Wells was eulogized as "the great prophet of our time" and "a man whose word was light in a thousand dark places."

Ultimately, Wells's daring mission in his writing was not to predict, but to change the future. If he described destruction vividly enough, he hoped to make people take steps to avoid it. Disaster didn't have to be inevitable. Much violence was coming, but also the promise of enlightenment. Pockets of people could survive, and a visionary elite could take control and form a world state. By the mid-twenty-first century, he hoped, we might even have a peaceful world adorned with techno-scientific marvels. Humanity *would* destroy itself and the world . . . unless some dramatic change took place.

When asked near the end of his life how his gravestone should read, he said: "Damn you all: I told you so."

Edgar Cayce

"Sleep now, and we will help you."

THE MOST DOCUMENTED
PSYCHIC (1877-1945) OF THE
TWENTIETH CENTURY,
HAILED AS "AMERICA'S SLEEPING PROPHET"
FOR THE ACCURATE PREDICTIONS
HE MADE WHILE ASLEEP

During the lifetime of Edgar Cayce, the United States transformed itself. Miraculous labor-saving machines were everywhere. And they could seemingly do anything: transport you from one place to another with ease, sew and wash your clothes, vacuum your house, type your letters—even manufacture more machines. By 1945, industrial technology had made the United States the world's superpower, with the highest standard of living anywhere.

In Kentucky, Edgar Cayce lived in a world apart from high-tech progress. He was shy, good-natured, kind of a bumbler. His thoughts were like no one else's. Certainly no one has ever been able to explain the unnerving accuracy of his visions.

"The Thing"

Cayce (pronounced like "Casey") was born in 1877 to a fundamentalist Christian family. Thought to be learning impaired, Cayce at age nine was in trouble at school for his lack of headway with spelling. One night, he later claimed, he heard a voice: "Sleep now, and we will help you." He dozed off with the spelling book under his head. When he woke, he suddenly knew every lesson in the book. After this none of the other children could keep up with him in school.

Nevertheless, Cayce left after eighth grade and tried numerous careers, without much success. Gradually he became more appreciative of his unusual powers, though he rarely called himself a psychic. He referred instead to "the thing I do." At twenty-four he went into his first trance to help another person, but not until age forty-six did he decide to make such trances his life's work.

The "thing" Cayce did happened on the plain green couch in his office. Twice a day, he would loosen his belt, tie, and shoelaces, then lie down and pull an afghan over him. Step by step he took himself into unconsciousness, where he saw a flash of brilliant white light. While in a trance, he could respond to any question asked by individuals from any walk of life. His wife, Gertrude, would read to him from the mail, and a secretary would take notes. He breathed deeply and moved slowly, concentrating hard, lips pursed. He would become more and more concise, as if without a minute to spare, until he would say, "We are through for the present."

Gertrude would direct him to wake up. He would open his eyes, stretch, and ask, "Did you get anything?" Then, over a snack of milk and crackers, he'd go over the transcripts: Oddly enough, Cayce had no recall of what he'd just said.

All of the transcripts of his readings are internally consistent and logical. While in a trance, he could speak languages he'd never learned, diagnose conditions for people he'd never met, use technical terms unknown to him in his waking life, and act as though he had encyclopedic knowledge. Believing that his gift was in direct service to those in need, he concentrated on helping people medically. Nearly 70 percent of the fourteen thousand readings Cayce gave involved diseases and treatments, often for patients whom doctors had declared incurable. Without medical training, Cayce prescribed combinations of natural ingredients to make healing formulas.

Usually he spoke in a firm, formal style. Sometimes he made offhand, homey comments about what he was seeing: "Right pretty pajamas" or "What a muddle-puddle, yet what a beautiful, talented soul!" Sudden interruptions would make him leap to his feet, disoriented. If he saw something violent (as when he was asked to locate murderers), he would be upset for days. "We haven't that" would be his abrupt response if a patient requested unrelated types of advice—asking how to get rid of warts and also about marriage prospects, for example. To someone with too many questions, he could be tart: "Do something for yourself!" or "Next you'll be asking whether to blow your nose with your right hand or your left." On rare days when nothing came, he would apologize: "It isn't anything I can control."

PROS AND CONS TO BEING PSYCHIC

By 1910, headlines about "America's Sleeping Prophet" were appearing. *The New York Times* declared, "Illiterate Man Becomes a Doctor When Hypnotized." Thousands of letters a week started pouring in. Children whose parents had sought readings about their talents and personalities became known as "Cayce babies."

And of course, people tried to find out his secret. A committee of experts once tested him. While he was in a trance, they shoved a pin through his cheek and peeled back the nail of his little finger. He showed no pain until he woke up, when he began bleeding heavily; his finger continued to throb for a year.

The closest anyone came to an explanation for his gift was Cayce himself. Someone once asked him during a reading for the source of his information. He replied, "Edgar Cayce's mind . . . has the power to interpret to the objective minds of others what it acquired from the subconscious mind of other individuals." In other words, he claimed to be tapping into the knowledge possessed by millions of people, including those who had died—an unlimited, universal source of wisdom.

Actually, Cayce believed that we are all psychic to some degree. "Mind is the builder," he once wrote. "The thoughts you hold create the currents over which the wings of your experience must go." He saw the mind as a particularly powerful tool in creating health and wellness. We should seek out psychic experiences, he thought, not for the sake of having them, but for our own spiritual growth and for serving others.

Cayce wasn't able to do much good for himself—his gift just didn't work that way. For years he refused payment. Yet he did know his own worth: When movie star Joan Crawford called and asked him to come at once to Hollywood for a reading, he replied that he could work her into his schedule . . . in a year or two. But he tried to duck from publicity, anxious not to establish a cult with himself as the subject of worship. He went bankrupt several times and was constantly in financial crisis, sometimes even with holes in his shoes. His wife was often ill, and one baby son died—and Cayce was depressed by being unable to help.

But sometimes his gift did come to his rescue as a parent. His son Hugh Lynn, for example, was annoyed that whenever he avoided his chores, or when he first smoked, drank, or skipped school, his father always *knew*. However, when Hugh Lynn almost lost both eyes after an accidental explosion, Cayce applied bandages soaked with tannic acid, against doctors' advice. At the end of fifteen days of this, Hugh Lynn could see perfectly and had no scars.

Cayce didn't need to be in a trance to read minds. He became a charming storyteller just to avoid picking up on people's thoughts, which he believed were none of his business. He loved to play bridge but said he couldn't, because he could read the other players' minds and the challenge was gone. He read the Bible straight through every year, but not many other books—he said that as soon as he would start one, he knew the entire text already, so the fun went out of it.

People in his hometown often treated him like a freak, though they seemed to respect him. Publicity about his work brought criticism, especially from those in authority. He did have fans, but the general public tended to be suspicious. All the technological and scientific advances of the last century were working to increase people's skepticism of those who seemed to be psychic. The medical profession had been quick to label Cayce an outright quack. Even he described himself as "very eccentric in many ways." Persecution from police was occasionally intense. Cayce actually did two stints in jail, one for practicing medicine without a license and one for fortune-telling.

In 1931, to give him a measure of protection and stability, some wealthy supporters financed the construction of a hospital for him in Virginia Beach, Virginia. There he established the Association for Research and Enlightenment, Inc. (A.R.E.). This nonprofit organization held conferences, operated a clinic, and cataloged his readings. The readings eventually numbered into the millions of words on more than ten thousand major topics, from how to get rid of pinworms to prehistory, from the value of peanuts to predictions about the future.

THINGS COMING TRUE

In April 1929, Cayce warned friends to sell every stock they had—accurately predicting the stock market crash of that October. His sound business advice made many people rich.

Two years later, in 1931, he was working in his garden when the hoe suddenly fell out of his hands. He rushed into his house and locked himself in his study. Hours later he emerged with reports of a coming world war in which millions would die. Throughout the 1930s, he gave accurate dates and descriptions of events to come in World War II—the rise of the Nazis and the countries that would become involved. He predicted—at a time when this was most unlikely—that Communism would end in the Soviet Union and that Russia would be "born again." Other events he specifically foresaw and described include the independence of India and Israel, the deaths of Franklin Roosevelt and John F. Kennedy, and the invention of the laser.

Cayce was not always right. At least once or twice, he gave a reading without being aware that he was prescribing treatment for someone who had already died. He thought Hitler's motivations were good at first. In 1933 he predicted an earthquake in San Francisco within the next three years, next to which the 1906 quake would be a "baby." This never happened. Parts of Alabama did not sink underwater in 1936–8, as he foretold. Nor did New York City slide into the Atlantic in the mid-1970s. And Livingston, Montana, has not become the financial capital of the world—so far, anyway.

His most famous wrong turn was predicting California's tumble into the ocean. Cayce left the date for this catastrophe unspecified, but other psychics studied his work and decided it was going to be April 1969. Many people panicked and moved out of the state needlessly.

DANGER AHEAD

For the years to come, Cayce saw extreme turmoil. Vast geographical changes on the planet—land shifts, earthquakes, and volcanoes—were supposed to be obvious by 1998 and complete by 2000. He believed that the sea level was rising. He thought this was due to drops in the earth's surface of thirty or more feet; but perhaps he was foreseeing global warming and the depletion of the ozone layer. In any case, flood damage would cause major food shortages in the United States and starvation around the world.

West Coast destruction would come first. Los Angeles and San Francisco would be destroyed; Arizona oceanfront property would no longer be a joke. New York City and the Connecticut coastline were going under, as were the coasts of Georgia, South Carolina, and possibly North Carolina. The Great Lakes would empty into the Gulf of Mexico. The only safe areas would be Norfolk and Virginia Beach, Virginia (where Cayce happened to live); parts of Ohio, Indiana, Illinois; parts of Montana and Nevada; and the southern and eastern portions of Canada. Many of the northern European battlefields of World War II would go under "in the twinkling of an eye," in addition to most of Japan. But new land would appear in the Pacific and Atlantic.

By 2000, democracy would spread throughout the world. China would become a fervent Christian country with a powerful democracy to rival anyone's. Russia would be a center for religious development, and the hope of the world.

In the United States, great stress between blacks and whites would cause race riots; and there would also come a revolution of the poor against the rich. Cayce believed that racial and gender discrimination had to stop: "Those in position [must] give of their means, their wealth, their education, their position."

Cayce urged Americans to take the lead in ending warfare. If civilization could survive, humanity could continue to evolve. Our psychic powers would increase, and improve daily life. Then, geographical destruction would not signify the end of the world but, in time, would allow the dawning of a "New Age" of enlightened behavior in an advanced civilization. (He was the first to use this now-popular term in 1932.) New cities would be built, where everyone had some relationship to the land. The future could offer, not destruction and hopelessness, but the chance for people to work together building hope and community for all.

Despite all the catastrophes, Cayce was actually quite optimistic about the future.

He predicted that he might return in 1998 as a possible "liberator of the world." Another dream had him reborn in 2100, in Nebraska (by then the West Coast), where he would collect evidence to convince scientists he had lived two hundred years earlier. He'd fly east, in an airship, to an island where workmen would be rebuilding a city that turns out to be Manhattan. Houses would be made of glass.

By the end of his life, Cayce was working harder than ever. He was getting four hundred to five hundred letters a day, doing eight readings in a row, and injuring his health. The final reading he did on himself warned, "Get out of the office."

After his death in 1945, at age sixty-nine, fans labeled him the "American Nostradamus." Transcripts of his readings have inspired over three hundred popular books. His herbal formulas are still widely sold, and many people consider him the father of modern holistic medicine. His organization, A.R.E., is more active than ever, with hundreds of study groups around the world.

Jeane Dixon

"Something dreadful is going to happen to the president today."

American psychic (1918-1997)
who made one of the most
sensational forecasts of this century . . .
then built a career on it,
with mixed results

The year was 1952, and the early morning mist was turning to drizzle. World War II had been over for seven years. Its greatest hero, Dwight Eisenhower, was getting ready to conquer Washington, D.C. and become the new president.

Jeane Dixon, a darling of Washington society, stood alone in front of a statue of the Virgin Mary. As was her habit, she was attending early Mass at St. Matthew's Cathedral. Mere rain would never keep her away. These predawn hours were her best—her mind was at its most receptive. She waited patiently, head bowed. Suddenly a picture formed in her mind. She described it later as a vision of a young man . . . with striking blue eyes . . . living in the White House . . . a Democrat who would be elected in 1960 . . . and would die violently in office.

MUMBO JUMBO?

Dixon relayed her vision to many of the well-connected friends of her husband, a leading Washington realtor. They included the publisher of *Parade* magazine, who printed her prediction in 1956. Four years later, with the election of blue-eyed Democrat John F. Kennedy, friends noticed her increasing panic. As 1963 approached, she even tried to reach him through mutual friends. One friend who had promised to warn him didn't, because she knew the Kennedys would consider Dixon's story "some kind of mumbo jumbo."

On November 22, out to lunch with friends at the Mayflower Hotel, Dixon didn't touch her eggs Florentine. Two witnesses heard her say, "Something dreadful is going to happen to the president today." The orchestra fell silent abruptly, and the conductor announced that someone had just shot Kennedy. Dixon was obviously overwhelmed. Friends tried to comfort her, assuring her that he would probably be all right.

"No," she insisted. "You will learn that the president is dead."

BULL'S-EYES

Dixon's forecast of Kennedy's assassination caused a sensation. It is generally considered to be the most predocumented correct prediction—that is, the one most publicized ahead of time—in history.

But Dixon was used to seeing the future. A few years after her birth in 1918 to wealthy German immigrants in Wisconsin, a traveling gypsy fortune-teller gave her a crystal ball. Dixon treated it as a toy at first, like a kaleidoscope. She assumed that everyone could see pictures in it like she could. She told her mother about a black-edged letter she saw coming in the mail, and days later a letter arrived with news of her grandfather's death. When her father was away on a business trip, she saw him buying a large black and white dog; he returned with a rare collie.

Dixon came to cherish the uniqueness of her visions, enhancing them with the practice of astrology. She learned astrology as a child, she reported, from a

Jesuit priest. During World War II, when everyone pitched in to help win the war, she donated personal astrological readings to servicemen as a morale booster. Word spread of her accuracy, and she started getting mail from others seeking help. Her reputation was so remarkable that, in 1944, she was summoned to the White House by the president himself, Franklin D. Roosevelt. She dressed carefully, in a black designer suit trimmed with crystal-ball-shaped buttons, with her own crystal ball concealed in a silver fox fur draped over her arm. She told Roosevelt he had six months left to live, which proved correct.

Dixon went on to predict the exact day of the partition of India in 1947, one month before it occurred. She correctly forecasted that Indian leader Mohandas Gandhi would be assassinated the following year. Newspapers took note. Dixon became a respected horoscope columnist, interpreting astrological signs to tell the future.

Dixon's career highlighted the love-hate relationship Americans seem to have with astrology. In public we tend to disdain it because it can't be proven scientifically. Yet many clearly think differently in private. According to a 1990 Gallup poll, over 50 percent of adult Americans do take comfort in astrology. The percentage could be higher—some could be too ashamed to admit it. Astronomy, or the science that deals with studying the stars, is what more educated Americans say they are interested in. But in the United States, there are currently ten times as many astrologers, or people who interpret horoscopes, as there are astronomers.

Dixon's list of bull's-eye predictions gave astrology a real shot in the arm at first. As early as 1952, she predicted the race riots of the early 1960s. In 1960 she saw the 1968 murder of civil rights leader Martin Luther King (though she didn't believe James Earl Ray was his real killer). In 1949 she saw Richard Nixon as president (he was elected in 1968), and in 1962 Ronald Reagan as president (he was elected in 1980).

The list of accurate forecasts goes on: the 1964 Alaska earthquake; actress Marilyn Monroe's suicide nine months before it happened; the fall of the Berlin Wall; the second assassination attempt on President Gerald Ford; a dreadful plague that in 1978 would affect thousands in the United States (AIDS began appearing several years later); a headline-making shipping accident (perhaps her vision of the *Exxon Valdez*'s oil spill in 1989).

In the years after her bombshell prediction of Kennedy's death, Dixon's influence became immense. A fashion-conscious socialite, she sailed from party to party in sparkly evening gowns—always with pockets to hold the business cards of those who asked her to pray for them. Attracted to the new medium of television, she appeared as a fast-talking TV personality. She got as many as a thousand letters a day, sometimes addressed only to "Jeane Dixon, U.S.A." It is not an exaggeration to say that, during her prime, more people were paying attention to her statements than those from heads of governments or just about anyone else.

TOTAL BATTING AVERAGE

Many skeptics continued to say aloud that Dixon was a nut. And as powerful a presence on the American scene as she was, she didn't help matters by making all kinds of goofs: China was supposed to start World War III in 1958. Russia would be first to put a man on the moon, she said, in 1965; but the United States was first, four years later. Nixon's vice president, Spiro Agnew, would rise in stature; instead he resigned in disgrace. Small potential scandals were brewing within the Nixon administration, but he would move quickly to set them straight and be remembered as one of the great presidents; actually he became the first forced to resign. Up until October 19, 1968, Dixon insisted she saw no re-marriage for Kennedy's widow Jacqueline; she married Aristotle Onassis the following day.

None of these other predictions came true: A woman president by the 1980s. A comet striking the earth in the mid-1980s. An attack on the United States by third world countries. Racial harmony in the United States by 1980. Peace in Northern Ireland by 1988. The Catholic Church split into factions over the issue of priests marrying. George Bush reelected president in 1992. Formal education all but extinct by 2000, with children educated at home instead.

She got so much wrong that there is even a term for the phenomenon. "The Jeane Dixon Effect" is said to occur when people get excited over a few accurate predictions and ignore the much larger number of inaccurate ones.

Her own explanation? Like the Oracle at Delphi and the sibyls of Rome, she blamed any problems on interpretation. "When a psychic vision is not fulfilled as expected," she said, "it is not because what has been shown is not correct; it is because I have not interpreted the symbols correctly." Also, more flamboyant than other psychics, she boldly named names and exact dates. She gave details that were easy to prove wrong.

Despite all the glitches, her name passed into common usage as a synonym for *psychic.* To protect her clients from the embarrassment of being associated with her, she kept their names completely confidential. But the list was rumored to include at least three presidents; First Lady Nancy Reagan (who later shifted her loyalty to a rival); many cabinet officers, senators, NASA and Pentagon officials, and other public figures. Her horoscope column was distributed to eight hundred newspapers and read by millions. Even as her reputation for accuracy declined (and most well-educated people would no longer admit to believing her), she reached a broad audience with the predictions she made in supermarket tabloids.

HER METHODS

Dixon may have been a giddy socialite, gifted at self-promotion; but those closest to her saw her as saintly. As a child she had dreamed of becoming a nun. In developing her career, she put in at least ten hours a day, working every day of the year except Christmas, with no vacations. A nonsmoking vegetarian teetotaler, she spent hours each day making nourishing soups and squeezing fresh carrot juice for blind and elderly people. She believed that if she took money she would lose her special talent. All earnings from public appearances were turned over to her own nonprofit charitable foundation, Children to Children, Inc., which funded education and health projects for thirty years. She had a habit of taking in runaways and pregnant teens. Besides her own pet, Mike the

MagiCat, her home was filled with stray cats and dogs, and her vet bills were extravagant.

Dixon's Victorian-style house held many books—but not one of them a book of instruction on psychic phenomena. She wanted it clear to all that she had her own style, fusing at least ten methods. Besides astrology, she used numerology (the study of the significance of numbers), dreams, mind reading, and listening to inner voices. She kept the crystal ball all her life. She also kept an incomplete deck of cards, from which she claimed to get "vibrations" about people once they had handled them. She felt that another powerful technique was to touch people's fingertips, especially with the tip of her ring finger on her right hand. She would ask to shake hands, as a way to get to know someone. Eventually, she couldn't go anywhere without people pressing her into a corner and holding out their hands.

She claimed that her power came from God and made use of prayer. Most predictions appeared during prayer and meditation. Sometimes they startled her at blank moments, like when crossing the street.

She once gave a delicious hint at what it was like to have a vision: "I felt suspended and enfolded, as if I were surrounded by whipped cream." She went on to explain: "I feel a peacefulness and a love that are indescribable . . . I feel that I'm looking down from a higher planet and wondering why others can't see what I'm seeing."

Eventually, Dixon was so well known that rumors of things she supposedly said would flash around the world, gaining strength even if they weren't true. One of the many false rumors was that all girls with pierced ears would die of a mysterious disease in June 1969. Another was that Martian hordes were descending to Earth to carry off children and teenage girls.

The most mail she ever received was after a false rumor that she had predicted the death of the Beatles in a plane crash in August 1964. Distraught fans by the thousands blitzed her with letters and calls, wanting to keep their heroes alive. George Harrison's sister called on his behalf to see if the group should cancel its August appearances. Dixon rushed to publish a statement that she actually saw nothing but continued good health for the Beatles, with no violent deaths. Grateful Beatles fan clubs around the United States named her "Woman of the Year." In the end, as it turned out, Dixon was proven wrong again—in the case of John Lennon's 1980 murder.

DIXON ON THE FUTURE

Dixon was as specific about our future as she was about everything else. She believed that the year 2000 was not going to bring the end of the world. The earth will be around at least another two thousand years, she believed. World famine will end. But a third world war will break out, and earthquakes will be increasingly common through 2037. Peace will come to the Middle East around the end of the twentieth century, and a descendant of Egyptian Queen Nefertiti will come to power, uniting the world. As it was during the time of the sibyls, Rome will again become the center of world culture and learning. A powerful religious figure will be associated with Manhattan. Canada and Brazil will be superpowers, as will Japan. Intelligent life will be discovered on a sister planet on the other side of the sun, and the Internet will be a way to reach people no matter where they live.

In 2030, a man who seems like a peacemaker will turn into a warlord with more power than anyone has ever had: "All the tyrants in history are mere children in comparison with him." He will disguise himself as a religious figure that the United States will promote as a world leader, but he will conquer the whole earth with the most modern of weapons instead.

Given Jeane Dixon's batting average, some of what she saw about the twenty-first century may come true—and much may not.

But it seems safe to predict that she will not be forgotten. At the time of her death, in 1997, Dixon was the world's best-known living psychic. Later that year, a group of psychics launched "Jeane Dixon's PsychicNet"—the first live astrological service over the Internet.

Marshall McLuhan

"What haven't you noticed lately?"

CANADIAN PROFESSOR OF
ENGLISH LITERATURE (1911-1980)
WHO PRESENTED HIMSELF AS
AN ELECTRONIC ORACLE FORETELLING
THE FUTURE EFFECTS OF THE NEW MEDIA

In 1945 Americans found it thrilling to listen to news and entertainment on the radio, a relatively new invention. Then, the following year, several thousand of them bought something they could listen to *and* watch: a television set. This new electronic medium was soon selling at the phenomenal rate of five million a year, and by 1955, most American homes had a black-and-white set. The rest is history: Today Americans watch TV one out of every four hours they are awake.

By the second half of the twentieth century, American life was increasingly high-tech. And instead of taking their cues from a source like the ancient Oracle at Delphi, many people were turning to a nerdy college professor obsessed with new technology.

The Power of American Students

In the 1950s, seemingly out of nowhere, Marshall McLuhan started issuing public announcements about the future. He was not a psychic reporting messages from divine sources. Rather, he was an incredibly observant thinker who analyzed the real world. He examined the new electronic age so closely that he claimed to see where it was heading.

But McLuhan's statements were cryptic and dense with meaning. In this way, he really *was* like the all-powerful oracle—to whom he compared himself. But despite how difficult he was to understand, he became more and more quoted. His words may even be more universally known today than they were when he died in 1980.

Little in McLuhan's first forty years hinted at the influence he would wield. Born in Canada in 1911, he grew up to become an odd, quiet professor of English literature. He wore mismatched socks, hats too small for his head, and either an ill-fitting brown tweed suit or a gaudy Hawaiian shirt.

McLuhan's first teaching job at the University of Wisconsin got him started on his study of American society. "I was confronted with young Americans I was incapable of understanding," he remarked later. "I felt an urgent need to study their popular culture in order to get through." As observant as only an outsider can be, McLuhan got tips to last a lifetime from his students. He spent years watching, taking notes, analyzing—and worrying.

Finally, he felt it was time to start warning others of what he was seeing. It seemed to McLuhan that people were numb—"like tulips," he said— in their blank acceptance of their surroundings. His goal became to shock us awake. And he had tons to say: He wrote thirteen books, six hundred articles, and seventy-five thousand letters, and made hundreds of hours of audio and videotapes. Eccentric, somewhat bristly in private, he appeared in print and in public as all knowing. His farseeing comments turned out to articulate the worries of many other people. Some of his expressions ("the global village," "the medium is the message") became part of the language. He quickly became famous around the world. Today, his ideas continue to stimulate artists and thinkers everywhere.

"The Medium Is the Message"

McLuhan passionately believed that the medium, or the *means* of communication, was becoming more important than the *content* of the communication, or its message. In other words, the new electronic media—TV, video games, movies, computers—were more influential than whatever they happened to convey. He credited TV—not its programs, just the very act of watching—with breaking up the straightforward lines of the way we think. He said that it immersed people in events. It brought all kinds of previously unconnected places and times together in high-speed simultaneity, an "all-at-onceness." In time, he believed, the new media would take over and reshape human existence.

McLuhan was nervous that people weren't seeing just how much would change. Like a sibyl, he used past events everyone would recognize to gain support for his view of the future. He pointed out that the civil rights legislation of the 1960s would have failed without TV—the broadcast images of African Americans fighting for their rights convinced others to help them win. Likewise, Hitler's rise in 1930s Germany would have been impossible *with* TV—people around the world would have grasped his evil intentions sooner if his speeches had been televised.

And who could know what "total and ruthless" effect TV would have on future events? It was McLuhan's nature to fear the worst: the fragmentation of America; the erosion of institutions such as schools and churches; and—as a result—violence in streets and homes.

He predicted that the various media were going to affect children the most. Attention spans would grow ever shorter. Dyslexia would increase—a result of eye muscles immobilized from too much TV. Already, thanks to the new speed of information, children's brains were literally changing. They knew things only adults knew about in the past—sex, war, violence, addictions, prejudice—experiencing several "lifetimes" before they even got to school. The new technology was shifting the human nervous system so much that kids were getting impatient with the "linear," or straightforward activities—like reading traditional books, for example. They could find meaning only in the "nonlinear," such as video games. They knew how to think in terms of overlapping lines of simultaneous actions, alternative routes a story could take, and multiple points of view.

Try to imagine your life for just one day without any electronic media. It wasn't so long ago that this was the way life *was*. As one of the first to examine the revolution, McLuhan warned, "If you don't study the effects of technology, you become its slave."

RISE OF THE INTERNET

What McLuhan said about TV made sense: "The world-pool of electronic information movement will toss us all about like corks on a stormy sea." The changes he predicted are accelerating. Dependence on remote controls has multiplied the colorful images we absorb. The number of TVs in the world has more than tripled since 1980, the year of his death. That same year saw CNN, a news channel, blanket the world. This unifying force dissolved boundaries and differences between people that had lasted for centuries. A year later came MTV, the highly influential channel for music videos intended specifically for short attention spans. It seemed to take McLuhan's description of TV as "music for the eye" to its literal extreme.

But McLuhan's observations became even truer of computers. Twelve years after his death, the Internet was widely available—the simultaneous sharing of electronic experience. By 1995, users had contributed enough material to fill thirty million books of seven hundred pages each. The fastest-growing form of communication in history, it is an unprecedented bath of information flowing into home, school, office. The Internet has created a community without borders. Users can live anywhere—supporting McLuhan's theory that big cities would wither away, no longer needed as work centers. When he said that every man would be his own publisher, he meant by way of copy machines. But personalized Web sites take that idea much further. They literally do give people tools to become publishers, at a pace no print publication can compete with.

McLuhan's view that the media will far surpass "any possible influence Mom and Dad can now bring to bear" applies especially to the Internet. It gives children an equal footing—the ability to interact with information without adult help, speak for themselves, get access to previously off-limits topics, and form relationships they never had before. Cyberspace is changing the structure of the economy, the development of communities, the way rights are protected, and countless other aspects of society.

The computer magazine *Wired* has labeled the worried professor "Saint Marshall" for his seemingly psychic ability to foresee this technology and its dangers. While some find the "information superhighway" intoxicating, others are noticing that it can be isolating, addictive, and a serious time-waster. Information continuously pours over us. It is immediately replaced by newer information, making it difficult to focus. McLuhan thought that the media would cause a serious conflict between "our claim to privacy and the community's need to know," which foretells the current controversy about privacy on the Internet.

The worst consequences McLuhan feared about the media are being hotly debated right now. Is the lightning-speed flow of information being worshiped as a new divine power? Does it make us less able to reason, quicker to resort to violence? Unless we take control and study the effects of the Internet—which many people are now doing *on* the Internet—we won't be able to diagnose what is happening to us, much less fix it.

SEEING EVERYTHING IN A NEW WAY

Many of McLuhan's less eloquent ideas haven't lasted. Once he patented a spray that removed the smell of urine from underwear, but he couldn't get any company to manufacture it. He thought women were "constitutionally docile, uncritical, and routine-loving." Still, they would take over government and business, supporting a class of male loafers and warriors. "The day of the storyline, the plot, is over" is an observation many would disagree with. They would also doubt his prediction that, in the switch from a print culture to a visual one, books would very soon become obsolete.

Lots of critics found him totally outrageous and made fun of him. His puns were annoying. He kept his pockets stuffed with new ones, scribbled on scraps of paper, starting every conversation with groan-producing jokes. Many, especially friends he would wake at any hour, found his oceans of talk frustrating. His meanings were not always clear or consistent—a student once kept track and pointed out twenty-eight contradictions in a half hour speech. When put down, McLuhan would snap back, "You don't like those ideas? I got others."

He confessed to friends that he was incapable of understanding his six children. (They got back by occasionally firing BBs at his precious books.)

Still, anyone who even had lunch with him reported being able to see everything in a new way. His favorite question was, "What haven't you noticed lately?" Businessmen and world leaders chased him around to get his advice. He charged General Motors a huge fee, then informed them that cars were a thing of the past. After Bell Telephone paid him, he assured them they didn't really understand the phone's function. A leading package-design house was told that packaging would soon be obsolete, that everything would be sold in bins.

McLuhan believed that oracles don't take sides, so he tried to keep neutral about the changes he predicted. Clearly, he wasn't good at it. His personal life obviously revealed his preferences. He read constantly (though he detested science fiction); disliked watching TV (though he thought it could be clever); spent little time at the movies (though he did make an appearance—as himself—in Woody Allen's *Annie Hall*). Sometimes he thought the electronic universe was actually a manifestation of Satan. (A devout Catholic, he began each morning at four by reading the Bible in one of five languages.) He believed the future held a big risk of mass terror: pain, violence, even war.

But resistance was as futile as backing up a car on a crowded freeway. Resenting a new technology cannot halt its progress.

SCHOOLS OF THE FUTURE

Since 1984 the Marshall McLuhan Center on Global Communications has awarded the Distinguished Teacher Award to those teachers who each year have developed unique and creative computer applications in the classroom.

This is a result of one of McLuhan's many anxieties. He feared that the "television child" has no future in an educational system oriented to old technology, like simplistic textbooks. In an age of information overload, there is just too much to learn. Traditional teaching methods don't adequately pass on this new material to children. As a result, children are less involved, less interested, less apt to ask questions, which McLuhan felt were much more important than answers. School is in danger of becoming unreal and irrelevant, a prison without bars.

McLuhan felt that life in the classroom has to start fresh, with new techniques and values. Teachers must plunge into technology and, by understanding it, turn school's ivory tower into a control tower. Otherwise, society will only see more dropouts and more chaos.

The rise in drug use among youth is one warning sign. McLuhan predicted that drugs would become so pervasive that laws against them would be futile and, eventually, dropped. He thought drug use had many similarities to watching TV, and pointed out how kids used a TV term—"turning on"—for taking drugs.

Oddly enough, even with all his nightmares about catastrophes to come, McLuhan couldn't help feeling a certain amount of optimism about the future. Humans were resilient and would adapt themselves. He expected the whole planet to turn into a joyous art form, full of richness and creativity: "To be born in this age is a precious gift, and I regret the prospect of my own death only because I will leave so many pages of man's destiny . . . tantalizingly unread."

McLuhan considered himself a messenger of information about our future. And he didn't want to be executed just because he brought bad news. "The truth shall make you free" was a Bible quote that he liked—and he had it inscribed on his gravestone.

Further . . .

THE ORACLE AT DELPHI

Goodrich, Norma Lorre. *Priestesses.* New York: Franklin Watts, 1989.

Panaiotou, Niki Drossou. *Delphi: An Illustrated Guide with Reconstructions of the Ancient Monuments.* Athens: Gnosis Publishers, 1993.

For information about Delphi today, see "Welcome to Delphi" at http://agn.hol.gr/hellas/central/delphi.htm

THE SIBYLS

Parke, H. W. *Sibyls and Sibylline Prophecy in Classical Antiquity.* New York: Routledge, 1992.

For Michelangelo's view of the sibyls, see "The Virtual Sistine Chapel" at http://oar.rm.astro.it/amendola/chap.html.

For a game about Rome in A.D. 205, where a main character is a sibyl, see S.P.Q.R. at http://pathfinder.com/@@es2MogcAm6TR5rLQ/twep/rome/intro/help/cast.html

THE MAYA

Coe, Michael D. *The Maya,* fifth edition. New York: Thames and Hudson, 1993.

Kaser, R. T. *Mayan Oracles for the Millennium.* New York: Avon Books, 1996.

For the most recent discoveries about the ancient Maya, see "MayaQuest" at http://www.mecc.com/mayaquest.html.

Other Maya-related online resources can be found at http://www.halfmoon.org/links.html

HILDEGARD OF BINGEN

Bobko, Jane, editor. *Vision: The Life and Music of Hildegard von Bingen.* New York, Penguin Books, 1995.

Flanagan, Sabina. *Hildegard of Bingen: A Visionary Life.* New York: Routledge, 1990.

For a collection of Hildegard web links, see "Hildegard of Bingen" at http://www.uni-mainz.de/~horst/hildegard/ewelcome.html

LEONARDO DA VINCI

Bramley, Serge. *Leonardo: Discovering the Life of Leonardo da Vinci.* New York: HarperCollins, 1991.

"Leonardo Da Vinci" CD-ROM (includes the Codex Leicester). Bellevue, WA: Corbis, 1997.

"The Leonardo Museum in Vinci" (in Italy) is at http://www.leonet.it/comuni/vincimus/invinmus.html

NOSTRADAMUS

Hogue, John. *Nostradamus: The New Revelations.* Rockport, MA: Element Books, 1995.

Ward, Charles, editor. *Oracles of Nostradamus.* New York: Scribner's, 1940.

For a list of Nostradamus links, see "Resources for Nostradamus Research" at http://www.alumni.caltech.edu/~jamesf/nostradamus.html.

To visit the Nostradamus Society of America, see http://www.NostradamusUSA.com/.

The related Usenet Newsgroup is "alt.prophecies.nostradamus."

JULES VERNE

Lottman, Herbert R. *Jules Verne: An Exploratory Biography.* New York: St. Martin's, 1996.

For the most complete list of Jules Verne links, see "Zvi Har'El's Jules Verne Collection" at http://gauss.technion.ac.il/~rl/JulesVerne/

For information on Verne-based movies, see "Filmography for Jules Verne" at http://us.imdb.com/M/person-exact?+Verne,+Jules

Subscribe to the Verne discussion group at http://gauss.technion.ac.il/~rl/JulesVerne/forum

NICHOLAS BLACK ELK

Black Elk, as told through John G. Neihardt. *Black Elk Speaks: Being the Life Story of a Holy Man of the Oglala Sioux.* Lincoln: University of Nebraska Press, 1979.

Petrie, Hilda Neihardt. *Black Elk and Flaming Rainbow: Personal Memories of the Lakota Holy Man and John Neihardt.* Lincoln: University of Nebraska Press, 1995.

For numerous links to American Indian sites, including many references to Black Elk, see "NativeWeb Home Page" at http://www.nativeweb.org/ and "Treaty Productions Homepage" at http://www.russellmeans.com/

H. G. WELLS

Foot, Michael. *H. G.: The History of Mr. Wells.* Washington, D.C.: Counterpoint, 1995.

Mackenzie, Norman and Jeanne. *The Life of H. G. Wells: The Time Traveler.* London: The Hogarth Press, 1987.

For a collection of Wells links, see "The H. G. Wells Smorgasbord" at http://www.olemiss.edu/~egcash/wells.html

For more about *The War of the Worlds*, see "Study Guide for H. G. Wells: *The War of the Worlds*" at http://www.wsu.edu:8080/~brians/science_fiction/warofworlds.html

For Wells-based movies, see links at http://weber.u.washington.edu/%7Eataraxus/revlinks/wells.html

EDGAR CAYCE

Bro, Harmon Hartzell. *A Seer Out of Season: The Life of Edgar Cayce.* New York: St. Martin's, 1996.

Stern, Jess. Edgar Cayce: *The Sleeping Prophet.* New York: Bantam, 1968.

"The Complete Edgar Cayce Readings on CD-ROM." Virginia Beach, VA: A.R.E. Press, 1996.

Headquarters for the work of Edgar Cayce, "Association for Research and Enlightenment, Inc. (A.R.E.)" is at http://www.are-cayce.com/

For Cayce links, see "Edgar Cayce Books International Database" at http://edgarcayce.com/

JEANE DIXON

Dixon, Jeane. *My Life and Prophecies.* New York, Bantam, 1970.

Montgomery, Ruth. *A Gift of Prophecy: The Phenomenal Jeane Dixon.* New York, Morrow, 1965.

"Jeane Dixon's PsychicNet" is at http://www.jeanedixon.com/

MARSHALL McLUHAN

Gordon, Terrence W. *McLuhan for Beginners.* New York: Writers and Readers, 1997.

Marchand, Philip. *Marshall McLuhan: The Medium and the Messenger.* New York: Ticknor & Fields, 1989.

"Understanding McLuhan" CD-ROM. New York: Southam Interactive/Voyager, 1996.

For numerous McLuhan links, see "The Marshall McLuhan Center on Global Communications" at http://www.mcluhanmedia.com/

For more, see "McLuhanlinks" at http://www.voyagerco.com/catalog/mcluhan/indepth/links.html

To get the "McLuhan-List" newsletter, see "McLuhan Connection" at http://www.mediaguru.org/Info.html

Subscribe to the McLuhan discussion group at "The McLuhan Probes" at http://www.mcluhan.ca/mcluhan/

Index